THE
RAWHIDER

CALIBER
B O O K S

Also from DOYLE TRENT

CHAPTER 1

He couldn't believe what he was seeing.

Not up here where few humans had ever been.

He reined up, pushed his hat back and dragged a shirt sleeve across his eyes. The bay horse stood quietly, glad to stop. Downhill from him, about a mile down, the country flattened out into a broad valley with a few pine and spruce trees and a line of buck brush along a creek. Up here, on the edge of the mountains, tall trees and boulders as big as houses covered steep hills.

She didn't look up. She sat on a fallen tree with her elbows on her knees and chin in hands, a slender young woman in a long wool dress and a man's denim jacket. A blue polka dot bandana covered the top of her long blond hair and was tied under her chin. Not another living creature was in sight. The bay's hooves had made little sound on the cattle trail that led down out of the mountains, and she didn't seem aware that anyone was near.

Aw, couldn't be. He was still hung over from drinking that Taos Lightning the night before with Old Josh. He was seeing things that weren't there. Yeah, that was it. He grinned a crooked grin and pulled his hat down.

Yeah, he thought, Old Josh was always telling wild stories, and now he had wild stories on his mind. Like a story about finding a beautiful blond young woman sitting on a log all alone in the rocky San Juans.

"Hey," he said, expecting the vision to disappear. It didn't disappear.

With a squeeze of his lower legs, he urged the bay horse on, drawing closer. Still, it didn't disappear.

"Hey."

She looked up then. Eyes wide. Fearful. Like a deer that had suddenly become aware that something dangerous was near. For a few seconds he thought she was going to jump up and run. If she did he'd know he was seeing things, and he'd have something to tell Old Josh the next time they got to swapping stories.

But he'd sound crazy.

What would he do if she ran? Follow her?

"Hey. You real?" He was grinning foolishly.

Then she spoke. At first it was a strangling sound, and finally some words came out. "Uh, uh, sir, I...I'm afraid I..." She got to her feet and stood with her hands clasped in front, a mixture of fear and puzzlement on her face.

She was real.

He stammered a little himself, "I...I didn't mean to scare you, ma'am. Excuse me. You lost or something?" She twisted her hands. "Yes. No. That is, I think I know where I am, but my horse got away. I...couldn't catch him."

"Oh," he said. But he didn't understand at all. Glancing around, he didn't see a horse. He wanted to ask what she was doing up here, a good ten miles from the nearest town of Cloudcroft, but he didn't. "You said your horse got away?"

"Yes. He went that way, back the way we came." She half-turned and nodded down the trail to where it wound around some boulders and disappeared in the lodgepole pines. "I must confess I did something rather stupid. I dismounted and stood here admiring the view and the horse walked away."

"Uh-huh. They'll do that. Some of them will." He stayed on his horse, about to volunteer to go after her horse. But she continued talking.

"I tried to catch him, but he walked faster. I ran and he ran. He actually held his head to one side so the bridle reins stayed from under his feet." She didn't seem to be afraid anymore.

"Yes. It doesn't take a horse long to learn how to do that. You

6

say he went into the timber there?"

"Yes, sir." She tried a weak smile. Her teeth were white and even, and she had dark blue eyes. He wondered what she was doing up here alone, but it was none of his business and he didn't want to ask.

"I'll go fetch him." He rode the bay around her and went up the trail at a fast trot. As he passed her she said, "I would appreciate that very much, sir."

His gaze alternated between the ground in front of him and the country ahead. The horse's tracks were easy to see in the dry dirt of the trail, and her foot prints were there, too. Only—a frown creased his face for a second— her tracks were going back to where she was waiting. Not ahead. She must have tried to run around the horse and head him off.

Oh well.

The horse wasn't far away. It was cropping the grass in a small park near the trail. A brown horse, it carried a well-worn side saddle with one stirrup and a padded leather hook for a lady's right leg. The horse raised its head and watched him approach, but didn't try to run. He rode up, reached down and picked up the reins and turned both horses around. "You don't look like a horse that'd leave a lady afoot," he said. "But who knows what some horses will do."

Leading the horse back to her, he saw she was still standing and looking downhill. "Thank you very much," she said when he handed her the reins. "He seems to be very gentle, but I'll be sure to hold onto him from now on."

He dismounted and prepared to help her on the horse, but she wasn't ready yet. "It's beautiful, isn't it?" she said. "I just love the mountains in the fall. The colors are really spectacular."

Not knowing what to say, he merely nodded and said, "Yes."

She turned toward him and held out her right hand to shake, man-fashion. "I'm Valerie Mitchell. I'm certainly lucky you came along. It would be a long walk back to town."

"Yes," he said again, feeling like a dummy, then added, "My name is John Wesley. John Wesley Budeen." He took her white soft hand but quickly dropped it, afraid of soiling it.

"I'm happy to meet you, Mr. Budeen." Turning again, she

pointed downhill and said, "I wonder who lives in that cabin down there. Way down there near those red bushes. Do you happen to know?"

"Sure. I do."

"Oh. Of course. I should have guessed."

"Ma'am." He didn't know how to ask but he couldn't contain his curiosity. "It's none of my business, but I'm wondering what, uh..."

"You're wondering what I'm doing up here by myself." She smiled, this time a real smile. Pretty. "I must confess I'm a little odd. I love the mountains so much I just had to rent a horse and ride up here. I found this trail and followed it until I came to this spot. I had to stop here and just take it all in. I especially love the aspens, the way their leaves are turning to gold. It's beautiful."

"Then you rented that horse from Barney Howser at Cloudcroft?"

"Yes. Mr. Howser at the livery barn."

"You don't live around here, then?"

"No. I'm just visiting."

He wondered who she was visiting, but he'd asked enough questions. "Well, there's a lot of country up there. An awful lot of country. Men have been lost up there."

"I know. I didn't intend to go any farther. I wouldn't have come this far if I hadn't found this trail. Tell me, where does this trail go?"

"It peters out about five miles up that way." He pointed uphill and to the east. "Beyond that ridge up there it's nothing more than a game trail. Cattle grazing up here made a better path out of this end of it."

"I see. Do you have cattle, Mr. Budeen?"

"A few. There's three of us running stock in these hills."

"Then you must know this area very well."

"Pretty well. I've chased cattle over most of these mountains."

"These mountains are what they call the Blue Range, aren't they?" Before he could answer that question she asked another, "What's over there?" And then she smiled again and added, "Excuse me, I'm asking too many questions, aren't I?"

She was, but somehow her smile made him want to answer.

8

"There's a town over there called Rosebud. It's about forty miles, I'd reckon."

"Oh. You've been that far?"

"Once. Over a year ago."

"How interesting." She looked into his face, her blue eyes showing interest. What she saw was a slender man a little taller than average in his late twenties. He had brown hair, a straight nose and a wide mouth. Leather stovepipe leggings covered his denim pants everywhere but in the seat and crotch. A faded blue cotton shirt was buttoned all the way up to his throat and a wide-brim black hat that had seen too much wear was pulled down to his eyebrows. Big-roweled spurs were buckled onto his high-heeled boots. "Well," she said, finally, "I'd best be getting back to town." She turned to put her foot in the one stirrup.

"Let me help you." He said it, but he didn't know how to do it. He didn't know where to put his hands on her.

She managed to raise her left foot high enough to get it in the stirrup. She was wearing high buttoned shoes with heels. He noticed with satisfaction that she held onto the reins while she reached for the stirrup. He took hold of her elbow, but he knew he was no help. She didn't need any help. Taking the padded leather hook in her right hand, she pulled herself up until she was sitting on the saddle with her right leg around the hook. Her long dress covered her down to the shoes.

Smiling at him, she said, "Believe it or not, Mr. Budeen, I've been on a horse before."

"Yes, ma'am, I can see that." He had to grin. "You got on that saddle easier than I could have."

"I'd rather ride astraddle. That's the way I learned to ride when I was a child in Illinois. But most people think that's not ladylike."

"I'd hate to sit on a horse the way you're doing it. I'm not sure I could."

"Oh, you could get used to it." She lifted the reins. "I must get back to town. Thank you very much, Mr. Budeen. You practically saved my life. I hope to meet you again some time."

He touched the brim of his hat. "It was my pleasure, Miss, uh, Mrs.—"

"It's Miss. Good day, sir." She the touched the brown horse with the heel of her shoe and it moved on, walking rapidly downhill.

He stood with his hands on his hips and watched her go. Finally, he shook his head, grinned and said to himself, "Old Josh ain't gonna believe this."

By mid-afternoon he'd found seven of his bony Longhorn cows and their calves and had pushed them uphill to a grassy meadow with a narrow creek running through it. The cows wore two brands, the connected JB belonging to the rancher he'd bought them from, and the W Bar he'd registered in his own name. Their calves were branded on the left side with the W Bar.

"It's too early to drift down," he said to the cows. "Wait 'til the snow flies. Until then stuff yourselves with this mountain grass. Get fat. It's gonna be a long winter."

He'd been talking to animals all his life, and now, living alone, he even talked to himself at times. When he caught himself doing that, he shut up immediately. He didn't want to go crazy.

In the late afternoon he saw more cattle tracks and followed them east over a hill and across a narrow, treeless valley until he found the cattle. A dozen steers and heifers, all carrying the Broken O brand. It was a big O split down the middle, belonging to Old Man Jenkins and his two sons. The cattle were prime beeves, ready for market. John Wesley left them alone and turned his horse toward home.

If he had as much as moved the beeves out of their tracks and was seen doing it he'd have been accused by the Jenkinses of trying to steal them. And the Jenkinses were mean, trigger-happy sons of bitches.

As he rode back toward the well-worn cattle trail he couldn't help thinking about the blond young woman. Valerie Mitchell, she'd said. Pretty. Talked like a woman with an education. Riding alone in the mountains a long way from town. Not the kind of thing most women would do.

When he reached the trail, another thought came to his mind and he spoke it aloud:

"That brown horse wasn't hard to catch."

CHAPTER 2

On his way back home he gathered his five horses and one mule where they were grazing on the bunch grass and ran them into one of two corrals he'd built of lodgepole pines. At one end of the corral was a long three-sided stock shelter, also made of tree trunks. At the back of the shelter was another pole corral with a stack of fresh-cut hay in the middle of it. A grey tarp covered the top of the stack. He off-saddled the bay and turned all the horses out, keeping the mule in one of the corrals. He'd ride the mule in the morning to wrangle in the horses. By alternating night horses and saddle horses he didn't have to feed them, just let them graze.

Except in the winter.

He'd learned during the one winter he'd spent in southwestern Colorado that it paid to harvest some of the tall swamp grass that grew along the creek and keep it handy to feed stock. One bad storm last winter had almost cost him everything. Four cows had died from starvation and exposure, and if spring hadn't come early that year he'd have lost more. His horses were walking skeletons. He could have hug his hat on their hips. If he'd had feed for his horses, and had kept them strong, he could have driven the cows back to the foothills where there was shelter from the icy wind and a little grass. As it was, they had drifted south, keeping their rumps to the wind, heading where the snow was deeper and the grass was buried. The horses were too weak to ride, and he could do nothing afoot.

Harvesting hay—cutting it with a scythe, raking it, hauling it to

11

the corral and stacking it—wasn't his favorite kind of labor, but he, by God, wasn't going to let his horses go hungry again.

He chopped an armload of firewood and carried it into his one-room cabin, built a fire in the two-burner cast iron stove and peeled a potato. No meat tonight. Spuds and beans. Needed to go hunting. The last deer he'd shot had spoiled before he could eat it all and he'd thrown away the rest of the carcass two days earlier. Winter was coming. The temperature was cooling down. Meat would keep longer now.

The gallon can that he kept coal oil in was nearly empty, so he decided not to light the lamp. He could eat and wash dishes by candle light. Candles were cheaper than coal oil. He had to do whatever was cheaper. At least he wouldn't freeze this winter. His cabin had a plank floor now. One winter on a dirt floor was enough. He'd also re-chinked the cracks in the log walls and added another layer of tarpaper on the pole roof.

A wry grin turned up the corners of his mouth when he thought about it. His kin, the people he grew up with, wouldn't have done all that. Uncles Luke, Markus, Wilburt. Cousins John Henry, Luke Junior, Jonathan. Anything that couldn't be done horseback wasn't worth doing. They wouldn't go to the spring for a bucket of water without going horseback.

Times had changed. John Wesley had changed. Had to.

He was up at daylight, running the horses in and picking a sorrel for his mount. But he didn't ride far. After a breakfast of flapjacks and blackstrap molasses he rode to Turkey Creek two miles south of his homestead. There he hobbled the sorrel, picked up a longhandled scythe and went to work, cutting grass.

Swinging from right to left. Swish. Swish. Watching the tall grass fall. Tiresome. Boring.

He stopped for a moment, straightened his back and used a shirt sleeve to wipe the sweat from his forehead. Then went back to work. Tomorrow he'd rake what he'd cut into piles and the next day he'd hitch the mule and the big mare to the wagon and haul the hay to his stack yard. He had to do it while the weather was dry. Wet hay molded in the stack and moldy hay gave horses the colic.

Swish. Swish.

His noon meal was beans and biscuits heated on the cast iron stove and washed down with water from a spring back of the cabin. A man couldn't live without meat. Not for long. Had to go hunting. Had to harvest hay.

He could have borrowed some bacon from Old Josh, but he didn't want to tell him his troubles. Josh had helped him enough. Showed him the spring and a place to build a cabin, showed him how to file a claim under the Homestead laws, sold him fifty cows. He'd even helped him put up his cabin, and bought him a drink of whiskey when he went to town. He was an all-around good neighbor. A hell of a storyteller. Old Josh Bennett had been a hunter, trapper, miner, freighter, and Indian fighter, and was now a cattleman. John Wesley had to grin around a mouthful of biscuit when he recalled some of the stories Josh Bennett had told.

His meal over, he went back to the creek. Swish, swish. It was close to sundown when he saw riders coming. He straightened his back again, bent backwards to get the kinks out, and watched them come. There were two of them. They rode along the creek from the east at a high trot, and he knew who they were before they got to him. When they rode up, they sat their saddles without saying anything. They stared at John Wesley. He leaned on the handle of his scythe and stared back. They wore six-guns in holsters on their right hips. John Wesley seldom carried a gun. Finally Old Man Jenkins said: "The hell you doin'?"

John Wesley had an urge to say something sarcastic. The Jenkinses were never friendly. But smarting off would accomplish nothing. He thought it over, then said, "Trying to keep my horses from starving this winter." Old Man Jenkins was short and wide-shouldered with a gray beard and little pig eyes. No one spoke for another long moment. A horse blew through its nostrils and stamped its feet. Then: "You're cuttin' our grass."

"Well, that's a little hard to understand, Mr. Jenkins." John Wesley shifted his weight from one foot to another. "I've been led to believe that this land belongs to the U.S. Government."

Ralph Jenkins, the oldest son, kept quiet, but his eyes never left

John Wesley's face.

"We been cuttin' that grass long before you squatters ever saw this country," the older Jenkins said.

The name "squatter" never failed to rile John Wesley. He had no use for squatters either. He was a cattleman, damn it, and having to homestead to own a piece of land didn't make him a squatter. Not to his way of thinking. But again he fought down the urge to say something sarcastic, and drawled, "That's hard to understand, too, Mr. Jenkins. When I came here a year ago last summer this grass hadn't been cut."

The squinty eyes squinted tighter. "I said we been cuttin' it and that means we, by God, been cuttin' it, and that means you, by God, better believe it."

They stared at each other. If it came to a fight, John Wesley wouldn't have a chance. He'd brought his Winchester .44 in case he saw a deer, but it was in a boot on his saddle. And even if he had it in his hands with a shell in the chamber and the hammer back he wouldn't want to use it. He didn't want to shoot anyone.

Finally Ralph Jenkins spoke, "You the one that laid them logs down over yonder?"

"Where?" John Wesley asked.

Nodding to the south, Ralph Jenkins said, "Yonder. You know where. What's the idee?"

"I don't know nothing about any logs over there."

"I'm bettin' you do. You fixin' to build somethin'?"

"Naw."

"I'm bettin' you are. You'd best remember, we was here first and we ain't gonna let no goddam rawhider squatters squeeze us out."

For the third time, John Wesley had to fight down anger. He looked at the ground, at the horizon behind the Jenkinses, and finally back to Old Man Jenkins. He swallowed a bitter lump in his throat and said, "I'm a cowman, Mr. Jenkins, and I've got a lot of respect for the Right of Discovery, as the government calls it. But when I took up a homestead here none of this grass had ever had any cattle on it. I'm the first to use this territory. The law says I've got a right here, and even if there weren't any laws, I'd believe I've got a right here."

The squinty eyes didn't blink. "The laws was made by a bunch

14

of shit-for brains idiots in Washington and they ain't worth a hound dog shit in these parts."

"Your ranch house is a good ten miles from here. How much country do you think is yours?"

"All we want. We're plannin' on buyin' some more cows and winterin' over here."

John Wesley could only shake his head. "Well, all I can say is I'm here and I ain't leaving."

"You're leavin'. One way or another, you're leavin'." Old Man Jenkins reined his horse around so hard the animal threw its nose up to relieve the pain from the bit in its mouth. He rode away at a lope. Ralph Jenkins followed.

With a sad shake of his head, John Wesley watched them go back down the creek, east, toward their ranch. It was an old, gut-wrenching sadness. He'd heard this kind of fuss before. Back when he was a kid he'd heard cattlemen cuss "Them goddam rawhiders," and he'd heard his uncles argue, "We've got as much right here as any damn body else. And if any damn body doesn't like it, tell 'em to, by God, come shootin'." No one came shooting.

John Wesley had never fired a gun at a human.

He went back to work, swinging the long scythe. Swish, swish. By sundown he'd cut maybe two acres of grass. He wondered how long that would feed six horses. Not all winter. He'd have to cut some more, then rake it, haul it, stack it. He'd heard of mowing machines pulled by a team of horses, but he'd never seen one. If he ever saw one for sale, it would be a good investment. If he had the money. Which he didn't.

Tomorrow he'd be back here, doing what he could to survive a Colorado winter.

That night, while he ate his meatless meal, he remembered what Ralph Jenkins had said about some logs. Someone had dragged or carried some logs to a spot somewhere south of the creek. Someone was planning to build something. Another homesteader?

John Wesley groaned aloud. Old Man Jenkins was right about one thing: too many homesteaders, too many people. Too much livestock would ruin the country for grazing. The law gave everyone who came along the right to a hundred and sixty acres. All they had to do was make certain improvements on the land. But the land couldn't support just everybody who came along.

If another homesteader had claimed a spot anywhere near, the Jenkineses would sure enough be fighting mad.

Someone was going to be killed.

CHAPTER 3

They called them rawhiders because they used cowhide to make everything from water buckets and wheelbarrows to rugs and beds. That was back when a million cattle ran wild on the plains of West Texas, and belonged to anyone who could catch or kill them. The rawhiders migrated to Texas from Tennessee and North Carolina during and after the Civil War. During the war, when the South tried to conscript them, they loaded their belongings in wagons and headed west to the New Land. And for several decades they lived like gypsies, in wagons, traveling in caravans, never staying in one place very long and never building anything permanent.

When the war ended and a market for cattle opened in the East, the rawhiders began accumulating cattle. They had an uncanny eye for an unbranded calf or maverick, and they got to be as handy with a catch rope and a branding iron as the Mexican border cowboys. Kids barely big enough to walk were playing with ropes and catching everything they could get close enough to, including Old Rambler and Grandpa. Beef was their favorite food. They never butchered their own. Everything was cooked over an open fire, cooked well-done. Most rawhiders were married and had three or four young ones before they were twenty-five. Wagons were their homes. They slept in them, conceived babies and gave birth in them.

John Wesley was born in a wagon, and he grew up thanking his lucky stars he was born in a Studebaker wagon. His daddy had traded a Shuttler for the Studebaker two weeks before he was born. And that, his mother always said, is why he grew a little taller and a little handsomer than his many cousins.

"Give me a Studebaker any day for healthy kids," his mother, Arabella, had often said.

But, she had to admit later, the Shuttler was better for continued good health. John Wesley's daddy took ill one day and died three days later. No one knew what he died from, but the wagon got the blame. He was buried on the Texas prairie with nothing more than a busted doubletree to mark his grave. Arabella didn't stay single very long. She married his daddy's divorced brother who already had four kids. Somehow, she never gave birth again. She raised John Wesley's cousins as if they were her own, but John Wesley was the only one she taught to read and write. He read catalogs, and when he was in his early teens he read The Bible. In fact, he was sometimes called upon to read The Good Book to the rest of the camp.

The rawhiders were often accused of stealing cattle. No one ever proved it and no rawhider ever went to jail for stealing. Yet, when word got out that the rawhiders were camped nearby, cattlemen, sheepmen, and goat herders kept a close watch on their livestock.

And years later, when John Wesley was twenty-eight and had drifted north to the Turquoise Basin in the San Juans, the reputation of the rawhiders caught up with him. It was Old Man Jenkins who was the first to know. The old gent had drifted up from Texas twenty-five years earlier and he recognized the rawhider way of binding everything together with whang leather. The rawhide strips were put on wet, and when they dried they shrunk and pulled everything tight. One of John Wesley's cows had died and he had skinned her while the hide was still good and used whang strips to bind a broken hub on his wagon. A rawhider never wasted a good hide.

"You're one a them goddam rawhiders," Old Man Jenkins had bellowed one day in the Uptown Saloon in Cloudcroft. "I know all about you. I seen your kind before. You're a bunch of goddam thieves."

Jenkins was carrying a six-gun on his right hip, and John Wesley was unarmed. But the young man couldn't take that kind of insult. Hands balled into fists, he stomped up to the old man. "Take that back," he said through his teeth, "Take it back or I'll knock your fat stupid head off."

They would have fought if it hadn't been for Sheriff Joseph Watkins. The sheriff got his paunchy body between them, his back to the young man, and said, "That's purty strong language, Mr. Jenkins. You oughten to accuse a man of bein' a thief unless you got proof. You got any proof?"

"No," the old man said, "but I know the breed. I seen 'em in Texas. You watch. His herd'll grow while mine shrinks. It happens ever' time them goddam rawhiders come around."

Sheriff Watkins then turned his back to Old Man Jenkins and faced John Wesley. "I was elected Sheriff of this here county, and I won't stand for anybody big-loopin' cattle. I don't want no trouble from you, you hear?"

The young man wanted to say something in defense of himself, but he didn't know how to say it. Finally, he muttered, "Aw shit," turned on his heels and walked out. That was about a year ago, after John Wesley's cabin was completed and he was as ready for winter as he knew how to be. He and Josh Bennett got together in town now and then and had a few drinks of whiskey. Old Josh could drink all night without laying out a dime. All he had to do was tell stories. Other patrons of the Uptown kept the booze flowing just to hear him. And the other patrons soon realized that Josh Bennett's young friend was a sociable sort, and they treated him with respect.

All except the Jenkinses. They never again picked a fight with him, but the hard glances they gave him, and the way their hands stayed near their six-guns when they saw him had to be taken as a definite threat.

Now, it appeared that more homesteaders were going to move into the basin. The Jenkinses wouldn't take kindly to that. And John Wesley, when he thought about it, didn't like it either.

"What can you say?" he muttered to himself as he washed his supper dishes. "Now that I'm here shut the gate and don't allow nobody else in? Naw, that wouldn't be fair. But dammit, there's just so much land and grass and too damn many people."

He spent three more days haying. If the winter wasn't too long and the snow didn't stay deep all winter, he'd have enough for his horses. The cattle would lose weight in the winter, but they'd gain it back after the snow thawed in the spring.

Riding a short-backed brown horse he headed south, across the creek, looking for the logs that Ralph Jenkins had mentioned. If it was a homesteader's work, he ought to see a cabin, tent, wagon, or something. He saw nothing, but noticed with satisfaction that the bunch grass and the shorter gramma was strong and plentiful. In a normal year this was a good place to winter cattle. Some years weren't normal. On he rode, eyes searching. At noon he had seen nothing man-made, and he circled back, keeping to the west. He rode over a low hill, through a half-dozen short pines, across a shallow draw, and up onto the benchland. There he saw the tracks. Someone had dragged something. It wasn't hard to figure out what.

Following the tracks, he found himself heading south again, and soon came to the logs. Four logs. Pine. Cut from one of the scraggly stands that grew down here in the basin. Dragged here with a team of horses and laid out in a square.

What the blue hell for? he asked himself silently. Is this the start of a cabin? There weren't enough timbers in the basin to build anything. Anyone who wanted to build a cabin out of tree trunks would have to cut down trees in the high hills, and carry them down here. Or drag them. That would be a hell of a lot of work. John Wesley hadn't had to drag timbers far to build his cabin at the foot of the Blue Range, but this was a good six miles away.

Out of curiosity he followed horse tracks to see where they went. The harness team had been led away by a man on horseback. Their tracks went south a few miles, then turned west and headed straight for Cloudcroft.

Reining up, John Wesley lifted his hat, scratched his head and reset the hat. "That do beat all," he muttered aloud. "Laid four logs in a square and left. Wonder if he's coming back? Wonder what the hell he's up to?"

His grumbling stomach reminded him he had missed the noon meal, and he turned his horse north toward his homestead. "Oh well. No use worrying about that now. If I don't shoot some meat pretty soon I'm gonna shrivel up like a dried pea." He rode toward home at a steady trot. "Yup. Got to go hunting." Then he realized he was talking to himself and shut up.

THE RAWHIDER

* * *

The buck was a fat one with a wide rack of antlers. It was grazing with two does on top of a grassy hill. John Wesley would take whichever he could get a clean shot at. Meat was meat, no matter which sex. He dismounted back in the timber and crept closer, bending low and trying to move without making a sound. One of the does heard him, heard something, but didn't know what. Her head came up and her ears fanned forward, listening. The buck had its tail to John Wesley, but the other doe was standing broadside, about a hundred yards away. He knelt on one knee and squinted down the barrel of his Winchester carbine.

Right behind the left elbow. She won't even feel it. He squeezed the trigger.

The loud crack of the rifle suddenly filled the woods and echoed back from a rocky ridge to the north. Two of the deer wheeled, ran, and disappeared over the hill. His horse, standing behind him, jumped sideways and snorted, its head up. The mule, carrying a crossbuck saddle, spun and trotted off a ways, then stopped. The doe dropped immediately and lay still, a .44 slug in her heart.

Shooting meat was the easy part. Now came the job that John Wesley had never liked but had had to do many times. First, bleed the animal. He went to it, lifted his skinning knife out of a belt holster, and with a feeling of distaste, slit the throat. He turned the carcass so the head was downhill. While it bled, he went to the mule.

The mule was still a little skittish from the gunshot, and John Wesley had to talk to it to get an axe and a yard-square piece of cotton flour sack out of a pack pannier. All right, he said to himself silently, it has to be done so get to it.

Back at the carcass, he rolled it on its back with the feet up, grabbed a handful of hide just ahead of the organs and made a long, crosswise slash with his knife. Straddling it, he slid the knife forward, splitting the hide from the first slash up to the brisket. He had once made the mistake of cutting through the stomach wall and got a gush of green muck right in the face. That was a mistake he never made again. Now he turned around and cut along the brisket to the bone and through the neck, opening it up and exposing the windpipe to the chin.

21

With a grim face, he clipped the windpipe and throat ducts off at the throat and stripped it all out to the chest, leaving the neck clean. Using the axe, he chopped open the brisket, exposing the chest cavity.

The heart, liver, and sweetbreads he wrapped in the piece of cloth. The kidneys he threw away. Kidneys were all right if cooked right, but first he would have had to boil the urine out of them. He didn't care for that.

While he worked he envied city folks who bought their meat from someone else who had done the killing and butchering.

Thankful that his knife was made of good steel and was sharp, he left the bladder attached to the organs, and made a deep cut to the pelvis and on to the hind quarters, exposing the bone. Then with another deep cut he removed the anus from the inside. Now he turned the carcass so the head was uphill, then cut all ties of the lungs and intestines from the backbone and rolled them out and threw them aside. Some coyote would find a good meal here.

The trick now was to get the carcass home and hung up to air out as soon as possible. He would skin it later.

The mule didn't like the smell of blood and John Wesley had to tie its head to a tree before he could load the carcass across the pack saddle. With everything lashed down, he mounted his horse, took the mule's lead rope, and started downhill toward home. It was sundown before he got there and nearly dark by the time he had the carcass hung high in the stock shelter where the cool breeze would reach it but the coyotes couldn't. His hands were bloody, but he, by gosh, had meat.

With a stomach full of fried liver, spuds, and beans, he slept well that night—most of the night. Early in the morning, just at daybreak, a strange noise got through to his consciousness. He lay still and listened. At first he thought it was a bear after his butchered deer. He lit a candle, dressed hurriedly, grabbed his rifle, and started toward the door.

Then a horse outside blew through its nostrils. A horse stamped its feet. It wasn't one of his horses.

For a few seconds he stood near the door, listening. A horse blew its nose again. He took two fast steps to the table and pinched out the candle. In near darkness now, he went to the one window and looked out through the bottom left corner. Riders were out there. He saw two of them sitting their horses in the dim morning light. He didn't recognize them at first.

A six-gun popped and a lead slug shattered the window glass and thudded into the far wall. He jerked his head down.

"Budeen," a man bellowed. "Budeen, come out here." He didn't move. His heart was in his throat now, and fear suddenly rushed through his body, leaving a weakness in his limbs. It was Old Man Jenkins and at least one of his sons. Probably both.

"Budeen. Get your ass out here or we'll shoot you out."

CHAPTER 4

Swallowing hard, John Wesley summoned his courage, raised up, and looked out the window again. There were three of them, all right.

"Budeen, you heard me."

"What do you want?" His voice was weak, and he repeated the question louder, "Whatta you want?"

"You come out peacefully and we'll take you to town and let the sheriff hang you. Don't come out and we'll blast you out."

"What? Why?"

"For cattle stealin', that's why. We finally caught you with your britches down. We found the carcass and we found where you buried the hide."

"I didn't...what're you talking about? That's a buckskin hanging out there."

"Haw. You think we don't know a beef from a buckskin? We found it where you wrapped it in a blanket and tried to hide it under your haystack."

"What? You're crazy. I didn't hide nothing under no haystack."

"Haw. You think we cain't see? You think we ain't got eyes."

"You're crazy. I didn't steal no beef. Or anything else."

"You comin' out?"

He thought it over for a moment. But only for a moment. "If I did I'd be crazy."

"Then we'll shoot you out, by God."

24

"Why don't you go to town and get the law? Let the sheriff settle this."

"'Cause it's our beef that got stole, that's why. Us Jenkins fight our own battles. You comin' out or not?"

"Hell no."

A six-gun popped. A bullet splintered what remained of the window glass and smacked the wall. Another pistol fired, and a rifle opened up, sending three bullets in rapid succession through the window.

John Wesley crouched below the window and tried to figure out what to do. The men outside guessed he was below the window and concentrated their fire on the log wall, hoping one of their slugs would find its way between the logs. Their aim was good and two bullets ripped through the mud chinks. One missed John Wesley by a yard, the other by only inches.

He had to shoot back. Couldn't just crouch there and let them fire at will. It would be broad daylight soon and they'd come crashing through the door. He had to do something.

Bending low, he went to the west wall and took down the old Army Colt from where it hung in its worn leather holster. He checked the loads and made his way back to the window. Rifle bullets were tearing through the cracks in the wall now, and pouring through the window. It would be suicide to raise up and shoot back.

It would be suicide not to.

He crouched under the window, and silently counted:

One. Two.

At three, he raised up, took a quick look, saw a man with a rifle, and fired two shots as fast as he could cock the hammer back.

The men outside concentrated their fire at the window again. He had to duck. "Damn," he muttered. "This ain't gonna do at all. Not a-tall. John Wesley, you got to get your skinny ass out of here."

There was no way out. One door and one window. Both on the south side where the cold north wind couldn't blow through. All the Jenkinses had to do was watch the south side.

For a moment, the shooting stopped. Without counting this time he raised up and took a quick look. Old Man Jenkins was standing fifty feet away with a rifle in his hands. Just standing there, making a good target of himself. The two boys were not in sight.

All right, John Wesley thought, if you ain't got any better sense than that you ought to get shot. But he didn't want to do it. He'd never been in a gun fight before, and he didn't want to shoot anyone. He'd like to retreat. There was no place to retreat. He had to shoot someone or get shot. Shaking his head sadly, he raised the pistol and drew a bead on Old Man Jenkins. And that almost cost him his life.

A rifle bullet zipped past him so close he could feel the heat from it. His shirt collar jumped like something alive. He dropped to the floor.

"I got 'im, pop," a man yelled. "I got the son of a bitch." Ears ringing, John Wesley fingered his shirt collar, the hole in it, and couldn't believe he was still alive. He blinked, looked at his hands, at the Army Colt in his right hand, blinked again. By some miracle he was alive. And he knew then that he had fallen for a trick.

Sure. Old Man Jenkins had stood there to draw his fire, knowing he would have to look out the window, stand close to the window, and show his face. He would have to raise his gun hand above the window sill. He would have to make a good target of himself. And one of the sons was hiding behind the wagon out there with his rifle sights on the window, just waiting.

It had almost worked. They thought it did work. They would come up to the window now and look in to see where the body lay.

Feeling shaky, but moving fast, he stood and fired two more shots through the window. Not taking time to pick out a target, just letting them know he was able to shoot. Crouching again, he pulled cartridges from the gun belt and reloaded the Colt.

"God damn it," someone outside yelled. "You missed the son of a bitch."

More slugs poured through the window, and two more ripped between cracks in the south wall.

What next, John Wesley? he asked himself. You're trapped like a coon in a cage. They figure you'll give up pretty soon and beg them to take you to town and turn you over to the law. That might work. It might not. The Jenkinses were here before Colorado joined the Union. They had always made their own law, and they trusted their law more than they trusted the government law. In their minds, stealing cattle was a hanging offense.

But dammit he didn't steal anything. What was it they said about finding a beef carcass under his haystack? Couldn't be. He didn't steal any beef and he didn't hide any carcass. And he didn't bury any hides. It was all put up by the Jenkinses. They wanted to get rid of him and they fixed it to make it look like he'd butchered one of their steers. If the Jenkinses hanged him, the sheriff might accuse them of a crime but he'd never get a jury to convict them.

The rawhiders stole cattle. Everyone said so. John Wesley was a rawhider.

All right, he did do some stealing once. Just once. But he didn't sneak around about it. He did it right out in the open. And it wasn't livestock he stole. It was money. A bank's money.

Gunfire from outside ceased for the moment, giving John Wesley time to ponder his past sins. He'd always felt guilty, and he wondered now if what he did then was catching up to him.

It happened right after he'd spent thirty days in jail in Silverton, New Mexico. Thirty days for punching a man in the face. If the man had been anyone but a rich Easterner he wouldn't even have been arrested. But the judge, that empty-headed politician son of a bitch who wanted to put the fear of the law into the working stiffs, just had to order him to jail.

"You will respect the law," the judge had said. Sure.

Thirty days. He thought he'd go crazy. Another week and he would have. When they finally turned him out he was bitter and angry. So angry it was easy for a man named Smith to talk him into robbing the bank. Helping to rob it.

But it was wrong. He knew that. He'd never do anything like that again. And he was lucky. Smith was dead, shot by a sheriff's posse. It was pure luck that allowed him to escape into the mountains. He vowed he'd never again push his luck like that.

He was sure pushing it now.

All right, he'd push it a little farther and get out of here. There had to be a way. Think. His eyes went over the sparse furnishings, all homemade. A wooden bunk with a grass-filled mattress was against the north wall. There were a table and two chairs made of small tree trunks, a two-inch board, and rawhide. A wooden cabinet was nailed to the wall over the stove. It was where he kept his sack of coffee, a few cans of food, baking powder, a sack of flour, and a sack of sugar. The west wall was bare now that he'd taken down the Army Colt and its holster and belt. The floor was made of two-inch boards with deer hides stretched across most of it. A black bear hide was spread next to his bunk.

He wished he'd built a window on the north side. But on second thought it wouldn't help. There were three men out there, enough to watch two windows.

He sat on the floor, on a bare section, and tried to think of a way out. There was no way.

Unless...

With a little more luck, he might be able to do it. He couldn't waste time, though. Had to work fast and keep an eye on that window.

On his hands and knees, he crawled to the bunk, dragged it away from the wall and grunted with satisfaction. Yeah. He'd cussed when the logs he'd dragged up to build the north wall were too short. At the time he could either have gone back up on the high hill and cut and dragged down two more or he could make do with what he had. He'd made do.

To do that he'll built the bottom part of the north wall in sections. Two long sections and a short one in the middle. The short section was about three feet long. Two logs high and three feet long. None of the logs were nailed in place, just notched and fitted. The cracks between them were filled with mud. He remembered how, when he'd chinked the walls he'd wished for some of that clay adobe from down south, but he didn't have it and he'd made do with the best dirt he could find nearby.

Keeping an eye on the window, he used his belt knife to pry some of the dried mud from between the cracks. It turned to dust. There was daylight between the logs. Now if he could pry a couple of those short pieces out of there...

A bullet smacked the wall only inches above his head. He flattened on the floor and looked back at the window. No one showed. Another shot thudded into the wall. They were standing back away from the cabin and shooting through the window. How long were they going to do that before they tried something else?

Lying on his stomach, he pushed, pulled, and lifted on one of the short logs. It moved an inch but that was all. It was wedged in too tightly between the other logs. He turned around and kicked at it with his feet. Same result.

Dammit.

The only way he could move it was to cut away one of the notches that held it to the longer log. With an axe it would have been easy. His axe was outside. All right, he'd whittle on it with his skinning knife. It would be slow, but if he had enough time it would work. Lying on his side, he started whittling.

Two shots came through the window, but they missed him by a couple of yards. When he thought about it he guessed they weren't trying to hit him now, just keep him in the cabin. He whittled.

If he could get one short log out of place, the one above it would be easier to move. He continued whittling until he had the notch cut flat. Now maybe he could kick it out of place with his feet. He turned around onto his back.

Then he realized that it was quiet outside.

What were they up to? And was one of them watching the north side of the cabin just in case? If so, he was wasting his time. He had to look out.

Again, he crawled on his hands and knees until he was under the window, then slowly raised up to where he could see out of a bottom corner. Uh-oh. Old Man Jenkins and one of the boys were pushing his wagon around to the front of the cabin. It was a light wagon with a busted hub held together with rawhide. The elder Jenkins was maneuvering the tongue to turn the wagon while his oldest boy was pushing. It was easy to figure out what they were up to.

They were going to get the back end of the wagon aimed at the cabin door, push like hell and ram the door with it. If they could get up any speed at all they would make splinters of the door.

He had to get out. Now.

John Wesley hurried back to the north wall, lay on his back and kicked at the short log. Stopped. He'd seen only two of them pushing the wagon. Where was the other? That wasn't hard to figure out either. The other one was watching the north side. The elder Jenkins could have used more manpower pushing the wagon, but he knew it was important to watch the other side of the cabin.

That ruined everything.

Unless...

Somehow, he had to get all three of them on the south side. There was a way to do it. Maybe. It might work and it might not. At least it was a chance.

CHAPTER 5

He checked the loads in his six-gun, then the rifle, and crawled to the window. The wagon wheels creaked outside. They were busy pushing. Now was the time.

Standing, he shoved the rifle barrel out the window and squeezed the trigger. He jerked the rifle back inside and fired the six-gun, fanning the hammer, firing as fast as he could. Not taking aim, just making a lot of noise. When the hammer of the six-gun fell on an empty cartridge, he holstered it and levered a cartridge into the Winchester. Fired again. Levered in another and fired. Did it again.

Now they were shooting back. Good.

Someone yelled, "Is he comin' out, pop?"

"Yeah. He's comin' shootin'."

That was even better.

In three long fast steps he was at the north wall, hitting the floor on his back, kicking at the bottom logs. The lower one moved. It fell out on the ground. Two more kicks sent the next one out.

His Winchester in his hand, John Wesley put his head through the opening. No one was in sight. He crawled out, half-expecting to hear someone yell a warning. No one did.

The youngest Jenkins had left his position and hurried around to the front to get in on the kill. The three of them were waiting there, expecting him to make a shooting run for it. He ran. But he ran north from the opposite side of the cabin, into the ponderosas behind it, uphill. Stopped.

He'd never get anywhere on foot. Had to have a horse. Standing behind a tree where he'd be hard to see, he studied the corrals and the stock shelter. His night horse was in the corral, and the other horses were out of sight, somewhere south. It would take a lot of luck to get to the night horse, saddle him, and ride out without being seen. There wasn't that much luck in the world.

But there were the Jenkinses' horses, standing tied to the other side of the corral where they wouldn't be hit by a stray bullet. They were out of sight of the cabin.

This is stretching my luck too damn far, John Wesley thought as he started moving toward the back of the stock shelter. How long would the Jenkinses watch the cabin door? How long would it take them to get suspicious and go around back? Not long. They weren't that stupid.

At first, John Wesley started to "Indian" his way, slowly, keeping out of sight behind the ponderosas. But he knew he had little time, and he changed his tactic. He hurried, making as little sound as he could, but walking fast.

He couldn't believe it when he found himself back of the shelter, behind the hay stack, but there he was. And still no sound from the front of the cabin. The three horses were tied to a corral pole by the bridle reins. He picked a blue roan with long legs, one that could run, and untied the reins. Then he slipped the bridles off the other two.

Mounted, holding his rifle and the reins in one hand, he waved his hat at the two free horses and grinned when they discovered they were free and took off at a high trot. The Jenkinses were wise now. One of them yelled something. Shots were fired.

But he was horseback while they were afoot, and they wouldn't shoot their own horse, and as he spun the roan around and booted it into a run, he yelled back at them:

"Go to hell, you sons of bitches."

Josh Bennett wasn't in his house, wasn't around anywhere. John Wesley didn't expect to find him this time of day. He was no doubt up in the high hills on horseback, catching his cattle drifting down and throwing them back up. That's what John Wesley ought to be doing—not running from the Jenkinses.

Well, he'd go on to town alone. He was hoping old Josh would go with him. Josh knew the sheriff and could talk to him. John Wesley had always tried to avoid lawmen, didn't like the suspicious looks they gave him.

Well, there was a time—one time—when he'd actually gone looking for a sheriff. Riding at a fast trot, he remembered every little detail.

That one time was a year ago last spring when he'd gotten tired of running and hiding and looking over his shoulder. He had to find out whether the law in Silverton, New Mexico, was looking for him, whether they'd ever identified the second bank robber. He knew it was an awful gamble, but when it was over he was glad he'd done it. He had ridden right up to the courthouse, tied his horse in front, and walked, spurs chinging, right into the sheriff s office. The sheriff wasn't in, but a deputy was. It was a deputy John Wesley recognized, one who had brought him his meals when he was in the lockup. The deputy gave him a hard look, but didn't say anything.

"Remember me?" John Wesley had said. "Is the sheriff around?"

"Ha," said the deputy. "What kind of bird don't fly?"

He'd grinned with relief. "A jailbird. I just wanted to let you all know I'm back in town in case anybody wonders what become of me."

"Thought we got rid of you. Thought you dusted out of here."

"I did, but I'm back. Be sure to tell His Honor, the jackass judge, I'm back and I'm not friendly."

"You better keep your goddam nose clean, Budeen, or you'll end up in the crossbar hotel again."

"Ha." He spun on his heels and left, feeling like a hundred pounds had been taken off his shoulders. He'd gone back to Silverton to find out whether the sheriff and his deputies suspected him of anything, and he'd found out. He was whistling a happy tune when he rode out of Silverton and headed north.

Now he was going to see another sheriff in another town. It was that or go back and shoot it out with the Jenkinses, and that was a no-win game. If he survived and they didn't he'd have a hell of a lot of explaining to do. And if there really was a beef carcass under his haystack, nothing he could say would convince a jury he hadn't stolen it and shot its owners.

It was about five miles by his estimate from his homestead to Josh Bennett's and another four or five miles to Cloudcroft. The courthouse was on the west end of town, the far end, and he rode his stolen horse the four-block length of Main Street to get there. Traffic on the street was light, two freight wagons with squeaky wheels, a one-horse buggy, two cowboys on horseback. Most of the business buildings had false fronts with porch roofs that hung over the plank walk. The street was dry and dusty this time of year. That would change soon. Soon it would be snow and mud. No one paid him any mind.

The courthouse was well-built of quarried stone, with a red tile roof and a marble floor. The sheriff's office was in the basement. He walked down a short flight of rock steps to get there, and was relieved to see Sheriff Joseph Watkins sitting behind his desk.

Watkins looked up under his shaggy gray eyebrows when John Wesley walked in. His gray hair was neatly parted in the middle and a thin red cut on his wide chin was evidence of a fresh shave. He waited for the young man to speak.

"I've got a job for you, Sheriff." John Wesley stood in front of the desk, holding his rifle by the stock and barrel.

"Yeah?" Watkins's plump body grew tense. He no doubt expected to hear that someone had been shot to death somewhere in his county.

It was a long story, and the young man didn't know how to start. Finally, "I, uh, I just got away from the Jenkinses. They tried to kill me."

"How's that? What happened?" The sheriff was listening with a tight expression on his square face.

The young man sighed, leaned his rifle against the desk, hooked his thumbs in his belt, and talked. When he'd told it all, the sheriff sighed too and shook his head.

"Is there a beef carcass under your haystack?"

"I don't know. If there is I didn't put it there."

"How about a hide?"

"They said they found one buried. I don't know where."

"Well," Sheriff Watkins stood and took his hat off a peg on the wall. He shifted his gunbelt and walked in his jackboots to the door. "I'll get a horse."

Neither man talked much. When they got out of the town limits, Sheriff Watkins looked back at the western horizon and allowed, "Might git a shower today." They followed a well-traveled wagon road a few miles, then turned off onto a less-traveled pair of tracks to Josh Bennett's ranch. There, the sheriff hollered, got no answer, and went on, now following dim wagon tracks.

The sheriff spoke again. "Reckon it ain't gonna rain after all."

The Jenkinses were waiting, the elder Jenkins and one of his sons. They had built a fire in the yard in front of the cabin and were cooking something. When the sheriff and John Wesley drew closer, John Wesley said, "They're helping themselves to my buckskin."

"That's the least of your troubles," Watkins said.

When they rode up, Old Man Jenkins faced them spraddle-legged, his right hand resting on the butt of his holstered six-gun. He said, "Git off my horse."

John Wesley dismounted. He felt like saying something sarcastic, but he didn't. The Jenkinses were dangerous even with the sheriff present. They could start shooting. Watkins dismounted, too.

"Mr. Jenkins," he said, "I've been told you fired some shots at this young feller. Would you mind tellin' me what for?"

"'Cause he's a thief, that's what for. He butchered one of our prime steers."

"Why do you say that?"

"'Cause we seen it, that's why."

"Where is it?"

"To home. My boy Ralph took it home before it could spoil. We waited here 'cause we knowed that jasper'd have to come back."

Sheriff Watkins' thick eyebrows pulled together and he looked down at the ground for a moment. Then, "You took the evidence?"

"Shore. Ain't no use lettin' a good beef spoil."

"Well then..." Watkins shook his head in exasperation. "How can you prove that this man stole it?"

"We seen it, that's how."

John Wesley kept quiet. So did Edson Jenkins, the younger of the Jenkins boys.

"All right," the sheriff said with a shrug, "show me where you found it."

"Over yonder behind that there haystack."

Watkins turned and walked in that direction. John Wesley went with him. The Jenkinses were right behind. Some hay had been pulled out from the bottom of the stack, making a large cavity inside. Drag marks were visible in front of the hole."

"Right there. That's where we found it."

Hoof prints, and boot prints of several different men were also visible. The sheriff squatted and looked inside the cavity, then straightened. "How'd you happen to find it, Mr. Jenkins?"

"'Cause one of our steers was missin'. We came over here to look for it. He wasn't home, but we found it in a minute."

Watkins pondered that and turned to John Wesley.

"Did you say you had a deer butchered?"

"Yeah, it's hanging in the shed. That's where I was all day yesterday, hunting and butchering a doe. That's what these two gents were cooking over there."

"Show me it."

The deer carcass was still hanging in the stock shelter were John Wesley had left it. It has been partially skinned and a chunk of meat had been sliced off the left side.

"Looks like it was killed in the past day or two," Watkins mused. "Mr. Jenkins, when you came over here to look for your stolen beef, was this hangin' here?"

Old Man Jenkins pulled thoughtfully on his gray beard, and finally answered, "Naw. Cain't say it was."

"What'd you do when you found the beef carcass?"

Nodding at John Wesley, Jenkins said, "He wasn't around, so we went home and come back first thing this mornin'. We caught 'im before he got out of bed."

To John Wesley, the sheriff said, "How'n hell did you git away from 'em?"

"I can show you."

36

"Oh, never mind. That ain't important." He turned to the old man, "Mr. Jenkins, how can I arrest somebody for stealin' somethin' when there's no evidence that anything was stole?"

Nodding to the east, Jenkins said, "The hide's buried yonder." He walked away in the direction he'd nodded. Everyone followed. Sure enough, a shallow hole had been dug in the ground south of the corrals, and a beef hide was wadded on the ground beside it. Jenkins picked it up, shook it out and said, "See that brand? That's the Broken O. That there's our brand."

CHAPTER 6

"How'd you find this?" Sheriff Joseph Watkins asked.

"Hell," Old Man Jenkins snorted in his beard. "It was easy. Any fool can see something was dug here. His shovel was right over there leanin' against the fence."

"Where's the guts?"

"The guts? How'n hell would I know? Maybe he et 'em. These rawhiders'll eat anything. Hell, maybe the coyotes carried 'em away."

The bushy gray eyebrows drew together again. "You went all over this place and found this hide and a butchered beef, but you didn't find the guts. Not even the Injuns eat all the guts. And I don't see any coyote tracks around here. Do you?" Watkins paused, thoughtfully, and continued, "When do you think the steer was butchered?"

"Coulda been day before yestiddy."

"Uh-huh." Sheriff Watkins walked slowly back to his horse, head down, thinking. Again, everyone followed him. When he stopped, he looked Jenkins in the eyes. "Somethin's mighty queer here. It don't make sense."

"Why don't it?"

"You said Budeen wasn't here yesterday and that deer wasn't there. That has to mean he was huntin' like he said. Now why would a man go deer huntin' if he had a fresh beef? Whatta you say to that?"

"He's tricky. Them rawhiders're the smartest thieves that ever lived. Ever'body knows they stole cattle, and nobody could prove it

38

on 'em."

"Whatta you say to that, Budeen?"

"It was planted. I never saw that hide before. And if there was a beef carcass under my haystack, somebody else put it there. I was gone all day yesterday."

The sheriff's pale blue eyes were fixed on him. "Who'd do that, Budeen, and why?"

"I don't know." John Wesley couldn't meet the sheriff's gaze at first, then he looked at Jenkins, at Edson Jenkins and back at the sheriff, "I'll tell you this, the Jenkinses don't like people claiming any part of this basin, and they want us off. Consider that."

Jenkins's hand went to his six-gun, and his gray beard bristled. "Are you sayin' we planted that beef and hide here?"

"Now just a gosh-danged minute, Mr. Jenkins." The sheriff's voice was full of authority. "Git your hand off that gun. If any shootin's done here, I'm gonna do some shootin' myself."

It was a stare-down for a moment, then Jenkins put both hands on his hips. "I won't stand for bein' accused."

"You accused him."

"I know what I was talkin' about."

"All right, all right." Watkins waved one hand as if to dismiss the subject. "Like I said, this whole deal is mighty queer. I'm not the judge and I'm not a jury. And I'm not a prosecutor. But it's hard to believe Mr. Budeen here stole one of your steers, drove it over here, butchered it, hid the carcass, buried the hide but not the innards, and went deer huntin'. If you'd a left the carcass where you found it, I'd at least have some evidence. That hide proves that somethin' was butchered somewhere, but it don't prove it was butchered here. Damned if I know who'd do it, but it's hard to believe Mr. Budeen here done it. If he had a fresh beef to feed his face with why'd he go deer huntin'?"

The sheriff paused, and Jenkins started to say something, but the sheriff waved his hand again. "Now if you want, Mr. Jenkins, I'll go way the hell over to Rosebud and talk to the district attorney for these parts. But I'll bet he won't charge this young man with anything. The DA is a politician. A politician hates to lose a trial. And if all this was told to a jury, he'd lose. Now whatta you say?"

The old man's mouth twisted, and he muttered in a low hissing voice. "All I can say is the goddam laws was made for the goddam politicians, and there was more law around here before this territory joined in the Union, and we shore as hell knew what to do with cattle thieves, and if we ever see this goddam rawhider anywheres near our cattle we're gonna drop 'im right there."

John Wesley's respect for the sheriff had gone up a couple of notches today, and now it went up another notch. Watkins wasn't impressed at all by the old man's threats. He said, "Now, I wish you hadn't talked like that, Mr. Jenkins. If I find this young feller backshot, I'll know where to look for the shooter." He shook his head sadly. "I wish you hadn't said that."

Jenkins grabbed the reins of the horse John Wesley had ridden up on and nodded at his son. "We're goin'. But if any more beefs turn up missin', we'll be back. And," he said over his shoulder, "we ain't goin' to any law." He and the younger Jenkins mounted.

Sheriff Watkins said, "That ain't smart, Mr. Jenkins."

Reining the roan around, Jenkins said, "What'd you do, arrest me?"

"Yes sir, that I would, Mr. Jenkins. If it took an army to do it, then I'd get an army."

With that, the old man socked spurs to the horse and rode away at a gallop. His son followed. Watkins watched them go, then aimed his bushy brows at John Wesley. "Like I said, young feller, this is mighty queer. Either you didn't steal his steer or you did it real smart. There ain't enough evidence to take to a court of law. But smart thieves get caught sooner or later."

He picked up the reins of his own horse, but before he put his foot in the stirrup, John Wesley held out his hand to shake. "I'm obliged, sheriff. Maybe there is something to this law and order stuff after all."

Watkins shook with him, put his foot in the stirrup and mounted. "It's not what it's s'posed to be yet, but we're gittin' better at it. Watch yourself." He rode away at a trot.

"Yeah, I'll watch myself." John Wesley spoke aloud as he watched the sheriff ride away. "It's hard enough to scrabble out a living without having to worry about getting backshot."

It took the rest of the day to repair the damage. First he saddled his night horse, wrangled in his small remuda, caught a bay, and let the others out. The bay was one he could trust on a picket rope, and he tied the horse on a thirty-foot rope near the spring where it could graze. He fitted the two short logs back into the north side of his cabin and carried bucketful's of mud from the spring to chink the cracks. Then he had to refill the cracks that the Jenkinses had shot out on the south side. The window glass couldn't be replaced. Glass cost money, and he was out of money. A piece of blanket would have to do. That made it dark in the cabin even in broad daylight.

There was just enough daylight left to finish skinning the doe. Swearing at the careless way the Jenkinses had cut off a piece of meat, he sliced a small steak for his supper. Not trusting the bay horse to keep from getting tangled in the picket rope during the night, he put the horse in one of the corrals.

"You don't have to eat all the time," he said aloud.

The steak was fried in bacon fat in a hot skillet. Feeling that he deserved something special after the day he'd had, John Wesley opened an airtight can of corn to go with his fried potatoes. When he finished eating and washing the dishes, he dumped a double handful of red beans in a pot, covered them with water, and left them on the table to soak. He'd cook them the next evening.

Before he went to bed, he pushed the table up against the door and put his rifle and six-gun on a chair within easy reach of the bunk. Then, while he lay under the blankets on his back, hands under his head, he again felt that awful, empty feeling. Lord, it was lonely living by himself on a homestead far from the nearest neighbor. Sometimes the loneliness ate on him, made him wonder whether he really wanted to be a cowman and spend the rest of his life like this.

"Huh," he snorted aloud. His cousins had all married young and never got lonely. The girls they married were nothing to brag about, but they were genuine female. Some knew only one way to cook, and that was to burn the hell out of everything over an open fire, and most took a bath only about once a month, if that often. But hell, his kin was used to that. They were raised that way. So was he. The doctor's wife in Springerville, New Mexico Territory had been horrified when she'd seen him. He remembered her saying, "Lord have mercy, how do you people live, anyway?"

He was eighteen then, and that stay with the doctor and his wife sure changed his way of living. It was a change for the better, no doubt about that. But now he was lonely.

"Maybe I'll go see Old Josh tomorrow, try to get there early in the morning before he rides off somewhere, or in the evening when he gets back. Naw, can't do that. Got to cut some more grass. Get what little is left along Turkey Creek, and maybe cut some of that wheat grass in the draw south of the creek. Maybe I can go visiting day after tomorrow. Maybe I can even go to town pretty soon. Maybe..."

He realized he was talking to himself and shut up.

It was two days before he went to visit his nearest neighbor. He left an hour before the sun sat on top of a rim of blue mountains far to the west, planning to arrive at Josh Bennett's house about sundown. By then, the rancher would surely be at home. He was.

He saw John Wesley coming, and stood in front of his stock shelter waiting for him. "Git down, John Wesley Budeen," he said with a broad smile. "Supper's 'bout ready."

"Evenin', Mr. Josh Bennett," John Wesley smiled back. "Thought I'd beat you at a game of checkers."

Still smiling through his short, trimmed beard, the older man allowed, "The day ain't come when you can beat me at checkers, but if it makes you happy to try, I'll let you. Feed your old pony some hay if you want to."

"Aw, he's been cropping his own grass for a long time and I don't want to spoil him."

Standing there in his baggy, dirty wool pants held up with suspenders, his shapeless black hat and boots and spurs, Josh Bennett said, "I got a pot of stew cookin', and it ought to be ready 'bout now. Come on in, and let's stuff our bellies. I ain't got no licker, but hell we drunk enough of that stuff in town a few nights ago."

"Booze is the last thing I need," John Wesley said. "I drank so much the other night I got to seeing things that wasn't there. Wait 'til I tell you what I saw."

They went in the house, a two-room, board and batten structure, with a rock foundation, a rock fireplace and a steep roof covered with split wood shingles. It had been built with pride and had once been home to a man and his family. Much of the furniture was homemade and plain, but the kitchen table was of hand-carved oak, and there were chairs to match. A genuine rug with a flower design covered the center part of the combination kitchen and front room. John Wesley had seen the bedroom once when Bennett had allowed him in there to look at an old cap-and-ball rifle that was hanging on a wall. The bed was a four-poster with a handmade quilt on it. Another rug was on the floor in front of the bed. A carved wooden dresser sat against a far wall, and on it was a picture of a happy family.

John Wesley couldn't forget that picture. It came to his mind often. Josh Bennett was smooth-faced when the picture was taken, and his wife was a pretty, brown- haired woman with a pleasant smile. Their child was about three, John Wesley guessed, with the same brown hair, wide eyes, a round firm chin and an impish smile. He'd had to ask about them. The answers he got were short. Mrs. Bennett was the reason Old Josh had settled down and built a ranch instead of wandering aimlessly around the Western states. She had died of pneumonia. The child was living with Old Josh's sister somewhere.

"If she'd been a boy I'd a kept her," Josh had said. "It wouldn't do for a grizzly like me to raise a little girl."

John Wesley would have liked to ask more questions, but didn't. He could see that his friend and neighbor didn't want to talk about it. Now he wished he could get another look at the picture. He wished he had a picture of his own family.

"Set," Josh said as soon as they entered the house. "We'll eat and then I'll beat the peewadin' out of you at checkers."

With a chuckle, John Wesley said, "I'll agree to the first, but this time we're gonna play a game called 'I Win.'"

The stew was beef, potatoes, beans, carrots, turnips, and even corn. Old Josh served it with biscuits that were a little stale, but still good with apple butter smeared over them.

"I cooked 'er last night and let 'er set overnight," Josh said. "That lets ever'thing mix."

"Takes a while to cook a good stew," John Wesley allowed. "'Specially in the high country. Seems to take longer to boil anything around here. Takes a good five hours to cook a pot of beans."

"It's this thin air. Water doesn't have to git very hot to boil. I've been up so high in the mountains, over to Cripple Creek, where you could almost stick your finger in boilin' water."

They ate and washed the dishes. Josh Bennett sat at the table, lit a corncob pipe, and said, "All right. Now. You've been itchin' to tell me somethin' ever since you got here."

A grin came over John Wesley's face as he sat on the other side of the table. "Yeah. I've got something that'll beat any wild tale you ever told. In fact, I've got two stories."

"Spill it."

"You ain't gonna believe this. You couldn't make up a better tale than this." He told first about his ruckus with the Jenkinses, and before that could settle in Josh Bennett's mind, he told about finding a pretty blond young woman sitting on a rock up in the high hills. He finished with, "I don't blame you if you don't believe it."

A few puffs on his pipe, and Josh allowed, "I can believe the part about the Jenkinses, but the blond woman must have come to you in a dream." He chuckled, "I use to dream about blond women myself when I was a young buck."

John Wesley chuckled with him, shook his head and said, "Yeah. I must have been dreaming. But...naw, she was real, all right. Maybe I'll see her again. Said she was staying in Cloudcroft."

"Sure, sure." Then the older man's face turned serious. "You got to watch them Jenkinses. They ain't nobody's friends. When I started buildin' this house they come over and said this was their country, they was here first and I had no right here. I made 'em understand I was here to stay. They ain't neighborly and they don't speak to me in town, but they haven't made no fuss with me. I figger it's because our ranches are about fifteen miles apart. Then when you come along and took up a homestead in betwixt us, they got to packing six-shooters ever'where they go and they look like it wouldn't take much to get 'em started shootin'. You got to watch 'em."

With that, Josh Bennett sucked on his pipe until he determined the fire was out, and laid it on the table. "Well, I'll get the checkers and we'll see if you got any smarter." He stood and went into the bedroom. John Wesley wanted to follow him in and get another look at the family photograph, but he didn't want to be nosy. The older man came back with a well-worn checker board and a box of checkers.

They played three games. Josh Bennett won all three. "The way to do it is think ahead," he said with a chuckle. "That's somethin' you young fellers have to learn to do. Think ahead."

Outside, he held a lantern while his visitor saddled his horse and mounted. "Come back anytime. I'll always put the stew on."

"Maybe I'll see you in town pretty soon, Josh. I've about decided to drive a couple of calves to town and sell them. Got to raise some eating money."

"Come by here and I'll help you. And I'll buy you a drink of whiskey."

The night was black, but the horse knew where it had to go to get the load off its back, and with its excellent night vision it didn't waste a step. John Wesley let the reins hang slack and his mind wander.

There had to be at least one John Wesley in the caravan, and there had to be a John Henry, a Luke, and an Ezekiel. Among the women there had to be a Prudence and a Patience. None of his kin called him John or Johnnie. It was always Johnwesley, spoken as one word. John Wesley Budeen. He was probably the only Budeen left. It was measles that took his mother. It almost took him. He was the first to get sick.

He was eighteen when his mother and stepdad carried him to the doctor's house in Springerville, so sick he didn't know where he was. Doctor Effram Jones and Mrs. Jones took him in and put him to bed. It was the first time John Wesley had ever slept under a permanent roof, but he was too sick to care about that. He would have to stay in bed for a spell, Dr. Jones had said, maybe a long spell. The caravan waited outside town until the sheriff used more authority than he had a legal right to and ordered them to move on.

John Wesley was given a bath and a botched haircut, and his "pigtail" of snuff was taken away from him. "It's a filthy habit," Mrs.

Jones scolded. "You were a filthy young man when they brought you here."

Hell, all rawhiders, men and wonnen, had to have their snuff. Snuff was almost as important as eating and drinking. John Wesley had gone around with a jaw full of snuff since he was ten. As for bathing, hell, nobody had enough privacy in a caravan to take a bath. It was hard enough to find the privacy to scratch one's ass, let alone to take a bath. Who cared, anyway? Mrs. Jones cared.

"It took me two days to get the stink out of the house," she had scolded. "You're a handsome young man when you're cleaned up and I can't understand why you don't want to stay cleaned up."

She was a good soul, and the boy learned to appreciate her. He even found himself trying his best to please her. She helped him to improve his reading and got him to reading everything he could get his hands on. At first he was too sick to miss his pigtail, and when he got better he agreed with Mrs. Jones and gave up snuff for good. He'd seen too many men and women with teeth and gums rotted out.

Then came the day the doctor said he was well enough to leave. His only clothes were the one outfit Mrs. Jones had given him. She had burned everything he had gone there with, even his run-over-at-the-heels boots. He had no money, no horse, no nothing. How in hell was he going to pay the doctor? Doctor and Mrs. Jones had been good to him, and he had to pay them somehow.

There was only one way. He got a job on the nearby Turkey Track Ranch, so named because its brand resembled a Turkey Track. It was a big outfit that covered at least six hundred sections of land. He was a good worker, and he took every paycheck to town and handed it to the doctor. Not until he had the doctor paid did he buy some clothes, including a pair of boots.

The rawhiders were not only good at catching and branding wild cattle, they were good at catching and taming wild horses, too. John Wesley, a quiet, even-tempered youngster, developed a knack for taming the wild ones. He was at the Turkey Track only a short time when the cowboss realized that and assigned him to break colts. It was a job John Wesley liked, and he soon earned a reputation in that part of the country as being a good hand with young horses.

But there came a time when he was restless and homesick for

the caravan. He drew his wages and lit out on a good horse and saddle he'd bought with his wages. He didn't find the caravan. His uncles and cousins had scattered, some working on ranches and some prospecting for silver in the Black Mountains of southern New Mexico. Too much of the land was being claimed and fenced. The rawhiders no longer had the freedom they'd enjoyed for several generations.

And that wasn't the worst news. His mother was dead. She'd died the day after he left Doctor Jones's house, and his kin couldn't find him to tell him about it. John Wesley blamed himself. He hadn't told anyone where he was going. He found her grave. It was nothing more than a mound of dirt on the open prairie near Silverton with a wooden cross at one end. Her name and the date she died were carved on the cross. No one knew when she was born.

As John Wesley stood over her grave he felt like blubbering. He couldn't stop a tear from running down one cheek. Finally, he mounted his horse, took one last look, and rode away.

The world had changed. It would never be the same. The rawhiders were history.

He was alone.

Well, maybe not. He had a home on the Turkey Track.

He went back there and resumed working with the colts. He was thrown and kicked, and he always had a sore spot on his anatomy somewhere. But he was so accustomed to it he would have felt unnatural without it. At times he had an urge to drift, to see more of the country. But he pushed it out of his mind. It would be foolish to leave the Turkey Track. That's what he kept telling himself.

Until that rich Eastern son of a bitch came along.

CHAPTER 7

The days were shorter and the nights were colder, and when John Wesley found a thin sheet of ice around his spring one morning he knew winter wasn't far ahead. He wasn't looking forward to it. The winters were long and sometimes harsh.

And lonely.

His horses had started growing their long winter hair, and it didn't take much for them to work up a sweat. The sorrel was sweating now as it climbed the steep trail north of the homestead. The trail was the one where he'd found the blond girl. Valerie Mitchell was her name. He wondered if she was still in town. He'd find out soon.

An even dozen of his cows were grazing not far north of the trail, and ten of them had calves at their sides. Were the other two cows permanently barren or did they just not get bred? He'd find out next spring. If they didn't calve in the spring he'd sell them for beef. The calves were grazing too, and were plenty big enough to wean. A longhorn bull was grazing with them, and he didn't like the looks of the man on a horse. He shook his horns, pawed the ground and watched the visitor with a threatening eye. John Wesley went around him, giving him plenty of room, cut out two of the cows with steer calves, and pushed them downhill, toward the trail.

The cows and calves didn't want to leave the rest of the bunch and tried to turn back, but the sorrel gelding was wise to the ways of cattle and out maneuvered them and kept them going downhill. The rider gave the horse a slack rein and chuckled at how well it performed. "Atta boy. Sic 'em."

Back at the homestead, he cut the cows into one of the corrals and shut the gate on them, leaving the calves outside. The animals bawled for each other, and John Wesley felt a little pity. But not much. The calves didn't need their mothers anymore and it would have been a matter of time until the cows started kicking them away.

Dogies, the calves could be called, now that they were being weaned.

"It's a hard world," John Wesley said. "I didn't plan it this way. I'm only trying to live in it."

The calves didn't have much longer to live.

By morning they were grazing a hundred yards from the corral. John Wesley caught a fresh horse, got them together, and started them on the trail to town. Nothing was harder to handle than calves without their mothers, and by the time he got them to Josh Bennett's ranch he had nearly ridden his horse down, keeping them together and moving in the direction he wanted to go. The calves were exhausted, too, with their tongues hanging out and slobber stringing from their open mouths.

Old Josh saw them coming. He loaned his neighbor a fresh horse and saddled one for himself. "I'll go along and help you. Hell, them brutes're gonna be dead by the time you get 'em to town unless we can get 'em there without chousin' 'em anymore."

"I was thinking I might have to nighthawk them around here somewhere and drive them the rest of the way in the morning. But if you want to help, we can get them to town and keep them healthy, too."

"Hell, the minute you looked the other way, them brutes'd head right back to where they saw their mommas last."

"I know it. I'd be in a fix if you hadn't been home."

"Hell, you helped me last spring, helped me gather my cattle and drive 'em up to the hills."

"Tell you what, when I sell them I'll buy you a beer or somethin'."

"I'll settle for that."

With two riders behind them, the calves stayed together. The men let them take their time and graze a little when they wanted to. They were looking healthier by the time they got to the outskirts of Cloudcroft. Within twenty minutes, John Wesley had sold one, and soon after he got the other to the livery pens he sold it, too.

"How much you askin', mister?"

"Thirteen bucks."

"Thirteen bucks? Shit, I can get a elk for nothin'."

"It'd take you two or three days, maybe longer. And maybe your family likes beef better."

The man walked away, muttering, "Shit, it takes me a whole week of packin' lumber to make thirteen bucks. More'n a week."

But the next man who came along bought the calf. He told Barney Howser, the livery owner, to feed it some hay and grain for a couple of days and he'd be back.

"All right," John Wesley said as he stuffed the money in a shirt pocket, "let's go buy a few groceries and then have a beer."

Their first stop was the Toltec Mercantile where John Wesley bought a sack of coffee, a few cans of food, and a slab of bacon. It was also where he again met Valerie Mitchell.

She came in while he was still choosing the cans he wanted, and he didn't see her until she spoke. "Good afternoon, Mr. Budeen."

He turned and his jaw dropped open.

"Or should I say good evening?"

Her blond hair was brushed until it shone. She wore a spotless blue cotton dress drawn snug in the middle, showing a small waist.

"Uh, good afternoon, Miss, uh, Mitchell." He realized he was stammering like a boy, and added, "I'm glad to see you got back to town all right."

A smile breaking across her smooth face, she said, "I had no more trouble. My rented horse was happy to be going home."

Josh Bennett came up then, carrying a bag of flour, and John Wesley wanted to punch him on the shoulder and say something like, See, I told you she was real. But instead, he said, "Miss Mitchell, I'd like to introduce you to my neighbor, Joshua Bennett. Josh, meet Miss Valerie Mitchell."

She held out her hand to shake, and Old Josh took it carefully.

"I'm very happy to meet you, Mr. Bennett."

He gulped. "Uh, pleased to meet you too, Miss Mitchell."

"Well, I'm sure you gentlemen have business to take care of." She turned toward the long counter that was piled with bolts of cloth, then turned back. "Oh, Mr. Budeen, there is something I would like to talk to you about, but it can wait."

"What is it, Miss?"

With a toss of her blond head, she said, "It can wait. We'll meet again, I'm sure." She turned back to the counter.

Outside, John Wesley stuffed his purchases into a pair of saddlebags and said to his neighbor, "You saw her. What did I tell you."

"I think I saw her. We can't both be dreamin'."

"You saw her."

"Hell. 'Stead of a beer let's have two beers."

They forgot about supper. The beer was good, and John Wesley was happy to have men around him. They stood at a long pinewood bar with a brass rail below it, stood between the spitoons, drank, talked and listened to the conversation. Being a quiet sort, John Wesley mostly just listened. The half-dozen customers in the saloon had heard about the gunfire at John Wesley's homestead, and they asked about it. He answered their questions, but briefly.

Someone said, "Old Man Jenkins thinks the whole basin belongs to him, and he's hell on homesteaders."

A rancher from the south end of Turquoise Basin said another homesteader had started building a shack down there, and the country was getting crowded.

"They just don't know how much country it takes to graze a few cows," he allowed. "And the only way to farm is to irrigate, and there ain't any water anywhere near the spot they picked."

"It's odd," said another. "But I reckon they're just plumb ignorant."

"They won't last long. They'll starve out before spring."

"How can anybody be so dumb they'll build a shack where there ain't no water?"

"Hard to believe, but stranger things've happened."

"Hear the U.S. Army's 'bout got all them Cheyennes and Arapahoes herded onto a reservation in Utah."

"They was a murderin' bunch. Nothin' they liked better'n to lift a white man's scalp. Or a woman's. Or, hell, even a kid's."

"Uh-hmmm." Josh Bennett had been quiet, listening, until then. He cleared his throat again. Conversation ceased.

"Uh-hmmm. 'Minds me of a feller I knew over to Colorado City," Josh began. "He was scalped twice by the Injuns and lived to tell about it. Well, once and a half, anyways. Uh-hmm. Throat gits dry when I talk."

Immediately, four men ordered more beer, and listened. Old Josh was about to tell a story. Josh drank half a mug of beer, wiped his short beard with a shirt sleeve and continued:

"Name was Judge Baldwin. Don't know why they called 'im Judge. He sure as hell didn't know nothin' about law. Run a herd of sheep along Monument Creek north of the settlement. Claimed to've been scalped by some Injuns down in South America once and had a big, ugly, red scar on the top of his head to prove it. Well, a bunch of them young bucks got to killin' ever' settler they could catch around there, and folks got so scared they brought their women and kids to a stockade they built."

Josh drained his beer mug and set it down with a bang on the bar. It was refilled immediately. John Wesley had had all the beer he wanted by then, and he just listened. Everyone listened.

"They had crops to tend and stock to keep track of, and in the daytime the men left the stockade and went on about their work, keepin' a sharp lookout for the Cheyennes at the same time. Uh-hmmm. I was workin' a minin' claim up on the Divide and was in the settlement to wet my swaller pipe and it wasn't none a my business, but I went along one day to see if I could help. Well, a few of us was on top of a hill north of the settlement and seen a dozen Injuns comin' from the east. We yelled and fired off our six-shooters and did everything we could to warn a couple of men that was down below us and about a half a mile away. There was a rancher named Everhart and the Judge. They heard the warnin' but it was too late."

The beer mug was drained, and the barman refilled it without being asked to. He put his elbows on the bar and his chin in his hands and waited for Old Josh to go on.

"Everhart socked the hooks to his horse and headed on a dead run for the settlement, but the Injuns had the angle on 'im. We'uns on the hill could see the puffs of smoke comin' from the Injuns' rifles, and Everhart was shot off his horse. The Injuns loped up and one of 'em got down and sliced off his scalp. When he held it up, drippin' blood, the savage sons of bitches all let out a war whoop. We couldn't do nothin' but just set there on our horses and watch. Then them Redskins spotted old Baldwin.

"Well, gents, I'll tell you, the Judge was ridin' a horse that was too little and too slow, and the Injuns was ridin' stole horses that could run. Old Judge tried. He even pulled off one of his long boots, the knee-high kind, and used it to whip his horse. Wasn't no use. The savages got closer and started shootin'. One shot hit old Judge in the back and he fell off his horse. The Injuns gathered around him like a bunch of magpies around a dead cow. But the Judge wasn't knocked out. Not yet, anyways. He got up and tried to fight 'em off, swingin' that boot like a whip, and held most of 'em back. But not for long."

Old Josh shook his head sadly. "One of them bucks got behind 'im and laid 'im out with a war club."

It was quiet in the saloon. The beer mug was refilled.

Josh Bennett took his time, letting the beer slide down his throat, smacking his lips. A man standing next to him couldn't stand it.

"Yeah? Yeah?"

"Uh-hmmm. They done just like they done to Everhart and started to cut off the Judge's scalp. But all of a sudden, the buck with the knife stopped and stared. He'd seen where the Judge'd been scalped before. Maybe it was a superstition, I don't know, but them bucks all took out of there like their asses was on fire. Wasn't nothin' we could do but go back to the settlement and git a wagon and go back for the bodies. Everhart was already turnin' cold. But the Judge? Gents, I wanta tell you, and I swear it's the truth, a bullet'd hit the Judge in the back, ripped through his chest and come out his jaw. But that tough old son of a buck was still alive.

"We hauled 'im to town, but nobody expected 'im to live through the night. Hell, he was chokin' on his own blood. A bunch of women and men sat up all night with 'im, watchin' 'im die. There wasn't no doctor anywheres near, and they didn't know what to do for 'im. I figgered he was a goner, and I hit the blankets. When I rolled out next mornin' they said he was still breathin' but he couldn't last much longer. Ever'thing that could be done for 'im was bein' done, and there wasn't no use me hangin' around.

"I'd spent what little yellow stuff I had and it was time for me to go back to my claim. A couple months later a feller came along and offered me cash money for my claim and I sold 'er and headed south for the winter. I drifted around for a few years, cowboyin', drivin' a four-up for Wells Fargo, diggin' for silver in New Mexico, and finally went back to Colorado City. I'm tellin' you, gents, I wouldn't a recognized the place. It'd grown like a patch of hogweeds, and there was a new town to the east a ways. The Denver and Rio Grande Railroad had laid track down from Denver and on south, and as fast as Colorado City was growin', the new town was growin' faster. Colorado Springs, they call 'er. A rich general built the railroad and platted the town, and some of his rich friends from England had built big houses there—and I mean *big*—and they brought their snooty English ways with them. They was all teetotalers and there wasn't a saloon in town. In fact, some folks called the new town Little London.

"Well, I just had to have a swaller of somethin' strong, and I walked into a saloon in Colorado City, and who do you think I saw?"

He stopped talking, and someone whispered, "Who?"

Josh Bennett looked at the faces around him. Everyone was quiet, listening. He drained his beer mug again, smacked his lips, and wiped a hand across his mouth.

"Judge Baldwin, that's who. Yep. It was him sure as shootin'. Big and ugly and loud as ever. He was an Irishman and he talked like it. The *r's* rolled off his tongue like buckshot pourin' out of your hand. When he got excited he couldn't hardly talk for his tongue kickin' out them *rs*. I had to buy 'im a drink just to see if he was real.

"Meanwhiles, the teetotaler town of Colorado Springs got to be a gatherin' place for the street corner preachers. They preached about sin, demon booze, and just about ever'thing, but 'specially booze. It wasn't long after I got back to town that they was usin' Judge Baldwin as an example of how bad licker was and what it could do to a man."

Another pause, and someone asked, "How's that?"

"How's that? Well, I'll tell you, and I swear it's so. The judge got drunk one night and staggered out on the street. That was the last time anybody saw 'im alive."

"Huh? What happened?"

"What happened? Well, I'll tell you. After all old Baldwin had lived through, bein' scalped by Injuns and bein' shot up so bad it took an angel of mercy to keep 'im alive, bein' half-scalped again, the son of a buck staggered around and fell in a well."

"Yeah?"

"Yup. The son of a buck drowned."

CHAPTER 8

For the next two days John Wesley rode hard, throwing his cows back uphill, keeping them out of the basin and saving the basin grass for winter. It was nearly dark when he got back to his homestead, ran in his remuda, caught a night horse, and turned the rest out. The bay he'd been riding rolled on the ground and scratched its sweating back, then got a drink at the spring and walked away. John Wesley chopped an armload of stove wood and carried it to the cabin. Stopped.

The door was open. Someone was in there. Or had been there.

Dropping the wood, he yelled, "Hello." No answer. He hollered again. He wished he had the old Army Colt as he walked carefully to the door and looked in. It was nearly dark inside, but he could see nothing that looked like a man. Only one way to be sure, though. He struck a match, held it head-high and looked in all four corners. There was no one.

Puzzled, he stepped outside. Too dark to search for footprints. Inside again he lit a candle and took a longer, more careful look. And then he noticed his mattress was out of place on the bunk and he knew before he looked that his money was gone.

Sure. How, he asked himself, could he be so dumb. Hell, under the mattress was the first place a thief would look. Should have hidden it outside somewhere. There were a million places outside to hide money, but no place inside.

Goddam. Who in Billy hell stole it? And—he sat on the bunk

and put his chin in his hands—what the hell was he going to do for eating money? Was it the Jenkinses? Or was it some drifter who stopped to bum a bite to eat, found no one at home and searched the cabin for money. He'd bet it was the Jenkinses. No drifter ever came around here. This place was a long way from any road that went anywhere. It had to be the Jenkinses.

Those sons of bitches. Those rotten, thieving sons of bitches. They'd do anything to run him off. Even steal his money.

He never locked his cabin. He didn't even own a lock. It would be useless anyway. If someone wanted to break in, he had all the time and privacy in the world to do it.

So what was he going to do about it? Ride over to the Jenkins ranch and accuse them? That would be dumb. In the first place they wouldn't admit it in a hundred years, and in the second place they'd shoot him on sight. He could take his rifle and the Army Colt and maybe get one or two of them, but not all three. The third would get him. What good is revenge to a dead man?

Or he could go get the sheriff. Joseph Watkins seemed to be a fair-minded lawman. Naw. They'd deny it, and he couldn't prove it. So, what could he do? Not a damned thing.

And that brought to mind the biggest problem: How was he going to buy groceries and stock salt and everything else a man had to have?

He'd hated to sell the calves. If he could have kept them until next fall, they'd have brought twice as much money. Damned if he was going to sell any more calves. He had the barren cows. If they really were barren they wouldn't be worth a dime more in the future, and they'd eat a lot of grass in the meantime. They were good beef and ought to bring enough money to keep in him groceries for a time.

Naw. They'd probably calve next spring and his herd would grow, and that's what he'd bought them for.

Bought them. Yep, he'd bought them fair and honest. Bought them from Josh Bennett and branded them with his own W Bar. But he'd bought them with stolen money. "Huh," he snorted, sitting on the bunk, "I stole some money and now somebody has stolen from me. But," he rationalized, "I didn't sneak around when nobody was at home to do it."

Still, when he thought about it and was honest with himself, he did steal it.

It was Smith's fault. Smith had talked him into it. Naw. He couldn't blame anyone but himself. A man was responsible for his own actions, not somebody else.

But, he thought, as he stood and went about the business of cooking his supper, he'd never do anything like that again.

Josh Bennett offered to lend him a couple of dollars. "Pay me back when you sell some more beefs."

"I'm hoping I won't have to sell any more stock 'til next fall when this year's calf crop will be big enough to bring a few bucks. Then I'm only gonna sell the steers. My herd will have some inbreeding, but it will grow."

They'd met horseback at the foot of the ridge that ran east and west between their properties. A cool breeze was blowing down off the ridge and both men turned up the collars of their jackets. The aspen leaves up higher were beginning to hit the ground, looking like gold coins among the pine needles. Down here, the grass was still green at the roots, but the tops were turning brown.

"Well then," Josh said, "you can work it off. I need help with my fall gather, and good help is hard to find. I hired a man to cut hay for me, but he ain't no good on a horse. I figure I've got about seventy-five good prime beefs to sell."

"You planning to drive them down to the railroad at Durango?"

"Maybe not that far. They tell me the Rio Grande built a side track and some stock pens east of Rosebud, and if that's true it'll take only three-four days to drive that many cattle around this range of mountains to the railroad pens there. I'll pay you to help me. A dollar six-bits a day, how's that? And I'll pay you to help me gather 'em. That'll take a week or more."

"The railroad did that? That'll sure save a lot of cattle herding. It's not far over the top of these hills, but it's too rough for moving cattle. If you can load cattle on rail cars east of this string of hills, that'll be the best thing that ever happened."

"Some day they'll lay track over here, but I don't expect it for a few years."

"Yeah, I'll help you. I've got to keep my cattle up there 'til the snowballs fly, but while I'm riding I'll cut out your young stuff and head them down this way."

"They'll git mixed up but that's all right. We'll separate 'em down here."

"Sure." John Wesley grinned a crooked grin. "Just don't move any Broken O stuff."

"Hell." Josh Bennett hawked and spat in the dirt. "If I see any of my cattle mixed with the Broken O, I'll damn sure cut 'em out. Anybody that don't like it can go take a flyin' jump off Old Baldy. I ain't gonna git in a shootin' match with them Jenkinses if I can help it, but I'll cut out my own cattle."

"That's what we'll do, then. I'll help you move your beeves to the railroad. That'll give me a few dollars to buy some chuck."

"I'll pay you for helpin' me gather, too."

"Whatever's fair. I only want to survive the winter. A year from now, if nothing happens, I'll have some beef to sell, and I'll be in better shape."

"How you fixed for horses?"

"I could use a couple more."

"Take two of mine. I've got plenty of horses."

For the next eight days, John Wesley was horseback all day every day. At first he left the Winchester at home—there was no comfortable way to carry a rifle on a horse—but he carried the Army Colt in a holster strapped around his waist. At night the temperature dropped to around forty degrees, but the sky was clear and the sun warmed up the world soon after sunup. The deer he'd shot was beginning to smell, and now he was carrying the rifle again in a boot under his right leg, stock forward. It was bulky under his knee, but he needed meat. Elk would have been mighty good, but the elk stayed far up in the mountains until the winter snow drove them down.

When he found JB cattle, he cut out the long yearlings and shoved them downhill, all the way down to the basin. One day, mid-afternoon, he saw two of the Jenkinses, the two sons, about a quarter-mile away. He was on a hill and they were below, popping cattle out of dense willows that lined a creek. He sat his horse and watched them. One of the boys saw him, reined up and pointed him out to his brother. They sat their horses and looked at him. He looked at them. Finally, they went back to work, yelling, slapping cattle with doubled catch ropes, trying to get them out into the open.

They could have used some help, and if they had been neighborly, John Wesley would have loped down there and helped. As it was, he could have been shot. Next day he met Josh Bennett.

The two men had each gathered a small bunch of cows and calves, and when they saw each other they threw their cattle together and let them graze on the side of a grassy hill. Both men got down and loosened the cinches on their saddles. They dropped the reins and let the horses crop the grass, too.

"I saw something mighty strange up there," John Wesley said, squatting on his heels.

"Yeah?" Old Josh filled his pipe, struck a wooden match.

"Can't figure it out. Looks like a cabin, but too little. There's four pole walls about six feet high and a pole roof that wouldn't stop water, and it's barely big enough for a cot and a barrel stove. A doorway, but no door."

"I seen one, too. Over east, just above my place. Not more'n two miles uphill from me. Just like the one you saw. Somebody cut down a bunch of trees to build 'er."

"Any sign of anybody living in it?"

"Nothin' in it. Dirt floor, and no door."

Watching his neighbor enjoy a pipe, John Wesley missed his snuff. "The one I saw is too little to live in anyway. What the purple hell could they be, Josh?" He didn't really want a pinch of pigtail, but he couldn't help thinking about it.

Two puffs of smoke came from one side of Josh Bennett's mouth, and he said, "'Minds me of somethin' I saw in the Black Mountains down south. Looked the same except the one I saw down there had a door. The door was fixed so it would slam shut and latch itself."

"Any idea what it was?"

"Yep." The older man sat on the seat of his pants and put his feet in front of him. He leaned back on his hands. "Bear trap."

"Bear trap?"

"Yep. Feller had it rigged to trap bears. What he done was he put some fresh meat inside the walls and left the door wide open. Then when one of them Silvertips stepped inside to he'p hisself to a free meal, the door slammed shut and latched itself."

"I'll be damned."

"All that feller had to do was walk up, poke a rifle barrel through the wall and shoot. Point blank. Couldn't miss. And then he skinned Mr. Silvertip and sold the hide. Sold some of the meat too. Some folks like bear meat. Me, I'd eat it if I had nothin' else, but there's lots of things I'd rather eat."

"Huh. Well, I reckon one way of killing a bear is as good as another. I heard the Silvertips are as big as a horse."

"Some of 'em are, and mean. Down in that country, in them days, a feller not only had the 'Paches to be scared of, the bears were just as mean. They'd tear a man's head off with one swipe of their paws."

"How about the Grizzlies up here? I've seen a few, and I gave them plenty of room. Most of the bears I've seen around here, though, are the little black boogers. They're more afraid of me than I am of them."

"There's still a lot of Grizzlies in this country, but not as many as there used to be. Too many people huntin' 'em. Some a them Eastern dandies think shootin' a bear is somethin' to go back home and brag about. I met a feller a couple years ago that made some money takin' a New Yorker on a huntin' trip. Got 'im a bear, too. A Grizzly. The New Yorker not only paid him for the trip but threw in a bonus for findin' 'im a bear to shoot."

John Wesley stood, went after his horse, and tightened the cinches. "Gonna get dark on us if we don't get these brutes moving."

Tapping the ashes out of his pipe on a boot heel, Josh Bennett did the same, got mounted. "Now that the railroad's come across the mountains, there'll probably be more of them New Yorkers come here. Them Easterners like to hunt."

The name "Easterner" brought an unpleasant memory to John Wesley's mind, but he shoved it aside.

The first light snow came in the night, and dark clouds threatened more the next day. Josh Bennett allowed he had all the steers gathered now, and all the heifers he wanted to ship. The two men cut out the beeves and shoved the rest of the JB cattle south of the Bennett Ranch. The few W Bar cattle mixed with them were turned loose in the shallow valley south of John Wesley's homestead.

"When we get back I'll have to wear down some horses keeping those brutes from heading for Mexico," he said.

"They won't drift too far. Nothin' can get over them Sangre de Christos in the winter. Tomorrow morning, soon's it's light, I'll load a pack horse with grub and our bedrolls and we'll start this bunch of beefs to the railroad." Josh Bennett looked at the sky. "If it snows now, we've got 'em all down here where the snow don't get too deep."

John Wesley was wearing a worn plaid mackinaw with a big collar. He turned the collar up. "Maybe the sun will come out tomorrow and we'll have a long Indian summer."

"Most years we do, but you can't count on it." With an apologetic look, Josh added, "I'd hire more help if I could, John, but it's the time of year when ever'body that can fork a horse has got a job. We'll have to take turns nighthawkin'. It'll be a hard three or four days, but when I sell 'em I'll have some cash money to pay you with."

"Well," John Wesley said, turning his horse toward home, "that's cow business. See you in the morning."

As he rode, hat pulled low, shoulders hunched inside the mackinaw, he knew there was something that neither man had mentioned, didn't want to mention. Driving cattle east, unless they went far out of their way, they would be going through Jenkins country.

John Wesley would carry both his guns.

CHAPTER 9

They had seventy-six steers and heifers, long yearlings, when they started east that morning under a partly cloudy sky. John Wesley noticed immediately that his neighbor was also carrying a rifle and a six-shooter. John Wesley had turned out all his horses except the one he was riding and the one he was leading. Josh Bennett was riding one and leading two. One of his was carrying a crossbuck saddle with a pannier on each side and a big sheet of canvas and four blankets folded and lashed on top.

"I can turn this pack horse loose and he'll foller us," Josh said. "I'm not so sure about my saddle horses, though. How about yours?"

"I'll hobble this one 'til we get these calves gathered," John Wesley said, nodding at his extra horse, "then I'll have to lead him. If I turn him loose he might go back home."

"These brutes shouldn't be hard to handle. They've been weaned for almost a year now."

The cattle hadn't scattered far during the night, and shortly after sunup the two men had them rounded up and strung out, heading due east, keeping Turkey Creek in sight. At times, they had to drop the lead ropes of their extra horses while they loped after a steer or heifer that didn't want to stay with the herd. But the haltered horses were easy to catch again. Two hours after sunup, John Wesley took off his mackinaw and tied it behind the cantle. With yells and whistles, they kept the cattle moving, Josh Bennett pointing them and John Wesley pushing from behind.

At noon they stopped long enough to eat some cold biscuits and bacon, and let their horses graze, then they were moving again, yelling, slapping their leather leggings to make popping noises. At mid-afternoon they saw one of the Jenkinses.

At first it was only one, but he disappeared, and a few hours later all three showed up. They sat their horses on a low hill a quarter-mile away and watched the small herd as it made its way slowly east. Josh Bennett left his position near the head of the herd and rode back to John Wesley.

"See 'em?"

"Yeah."

"Try to pretend you don't see 'em, but keep your eyes on 'em just the same."

"We're in their country now."

"Hell, we'll be in their country for at least two days, but we got a right to do what we're doin'. Let's try to ignore 'em and keep these brutes movin'."

The three Jenkinses followed them, but stayed behind. At sundown, Josh pointed the cattle toward the creek, held them up there, until John Wesley brought up the drags. The creek was in a shallow arroyo and lined with scrub oak. The cattle pushed their way through the brush, went right to the creek and put their noses in the water. Looking back, John Wesley saw the three riders behind them.

"Think they'll do anything, Josh?"

"Can't be certain, but I don't think so. If they was gonna cause a ruckus they would've done it."

"Maybe they'll wait 'til dark and start a stampede."

"They might. I'm keepin' my boots on and my saddle on a horse. If they start somethin', be sure who you're shootin' at. It might be me."

Their thirst sated most of the calves crossed the creek, pushed through brush on the other side and went looking for grass.

"That's just what they don't want," Josh Bennett said.

"My cattle croppin' their grass. But these brutes've got to eat."

"Be dark in a few minutes."

"Whatta you think, John, wanta build a fire and warm up a stew or eat a cold supper?"

"I don't want to be anywhere near a fire, making a target of myself, with those gunnies around."

"My sentiments, too. I'll unload the pack horse and hobble these animals we're ridin' and tie the other two back in the brush somewhere."

Supper was cold but filling. The older man had brought some fried steaks, and they made good sandwiches. John Wesley took the first guard, depending on his neighbor to spell him sometime around midnight. A half-moon gave him enough light to see most of the cattle. He reckoned they would graze until they were filled up, then lie down and rest and chew their cuds. If any of them drifted, they would probably try to go back to familiar territory. If they drifted east, so much the better. He kept himself between the calves and home. At the same time, he kept looking to the north, half-expecting to see riders looming up out of the dark, coming to stampede the cattle. He was south of the creek now, and the buck brush along the creek looked like a big black wall. The cattle were dark shapes in the moonlight. He stayed off his horse as much as he could, not wanting to make a target of himself, hoping he would look like another head of cattle. At times, however, he had to get mounted and turn back some calves that didn't want to stay with the herd. His mackinaw kept him warn in the chilly night.

Nothing happened. At midnight, he heard his neighbor calling his name softly. "John. It's me, Josh. Oh, John." He saw Josh ride out of the black buck brush. He mounted and rode toward him. "All's well, Josh," he said. "I think they're bedded down 'til daylight. They might get restless at first light. I'll get up then and come over in case you need any help."

"See anybody?"

"No."

"If I was a Jenkins and wanted to stampede these calves, I'd do 'er at night. They could be scattered all over the county by daylight."

"I'll put my saddle on my other horse and keep him handy. If I hear any shooting, I'll come running."

He had to hobble the horse he'd been riding and saddle the other one and tie him to a scrub cedar before he could roll up in a blanket. "I apologize, feller," he said to the horse. "Maybe you'll get some more grazing time tomorrow, or whenever we get out of Jenkins country."

He'd slept on the ground most of his life, and he was comfortable. But he wished he had the hearing of a dog and could sleep with his eyes open. The Jenkinses were tricky. They could wait until just before daylight to start something. If they shot Josh, he'd...well, he'd by god try to get at least one of them before they shot him.

Nothing happened.

When he rode out of the brush at first light he saw Josh Bennett riding at a trot around the south side of the bunch, letting the calves graze, but keeping them together. "Morning," John Wesley said. "They giving you any trouble?"

"Naw. They're too busy goin' after somebody else's grass. You et yet?"

Grinning a sheepish grin, John Wesley said, "No. I just woke up. Thought I'd better see if you needed any help."

"Naw. Go on back and grab a bite. Build a fire and cook some bacon. When you get the wrinkles out come and spell me."

He built a small fire of limbs he broke off the scrubs, heated an iron skillet and fried half a pound of bacon. While the bacon was frying, a gallon can half full of coffee was boiling. He ate bacon, cold biscuits and drank two cups of coffee, then went back to the herd.

"Looks peaceful," he said.

"Yep. Just let 'em crop the grass until I get my face stuffed and break camp, and we'll get 'em strung out again."

"Are you surprised the Jenkinses didn't show?"

"Somewhat. You can't tell what they'll do. They might kick up a ruckus yet."

"Maybe they won't. There's two of us, and when we get these calves out in the open, there won't be any place for a bushwhack. Their three guns can out shoot our two, but we'd get at least one of them. Maybe they don't want to pay the price."

"I was thinkin' the same thing. Hope you're right."

"But it's like you said, you can't tell what they'll do."

They saw one of the Jenkins boys again that day, but again he stayed away. Just watched. When they stopped for a cold noon meal,

Josh Bennett allowed, "I'm guessin' they only want to see that we keep movin' and don't try to set up housekeepin' around here."

"Yeah, well, we're gonna have to stop early and let our horses rest and graze. If we don't we're gonna be afoot." He sat on the ground with a sandwich in one hand and a tin cup of water in the other.

"You know somethin' about movin' cattle and keepin' horses strong, don't you, John?"

"I've had some experience with 'em, yeah."

"When you was a boy, growin' up with the rawhiders, you always kept a herd of cattle and horses, didn't you?"

"Yeah. My uncles were always selling cattle and trading horses." John Wesley grinned. "They never paid a dime for a horse, but they could trade the socks off anybody."

"It was good for a boy, growin' up that way. You learned to take care of yourself. I'd hate to try to cheat you in a horse swap."

"You learn." The memory of his mother, uncles, and cousins came to John Wesley's mind, and his grin vanished. He looked at the ground for a moment, then pushed the memory out of his mind and stood.

Leaving the older man to reload the pack horse, he switched mounts and went after the herd, yelling, whistling through his teeth, whirling a catch rope, and slapping his chaps. Soon Josh Bennett was in position, and they got the calves strung out and traveling again. Every few minutes, he looked back to see if the Jenkins boy was still there. He was. Always watching. No doubt, John Wesley thought, doing what his pa told him to do.

They made camp by Turkey Creek an hour before sundown, and took a chance and hobbled all their horses to let them graze. The country was nearly flat for at least a mile in each direction, and they reckoned they could see anyone coming in time to catch and saddle two horses. They built a fire—they couldn't hide anyway—and Josh Bennett opened a gallon lard can, swelled the contents, and put the can in the fire. Flames wrapped themselves around it.

"Beef stew," he said. "It won't keep forever, but it smells all right."

"A good stew tastes better every time you warm it up," John

Wesley allowed.

They ate, sitting cross-legged on the ground, keeping an eye on the cattle, keeping an eye on the horizon. The cattle grazed. Josh Bennett filled his pipe, lit it.

"Those brutes might git restless when they git their bellies full. I don't know, John, if we done the smart thing by campin' early and lettin' 'em rest."

"Naw. Hungry cattle are harder to handle than well-fed ones. Besides, you want some meat on these calves when you find a buyer."

"You're right about that, but hell, we might have to hold 'em up near the railroad pens for a few days. They could fill out then."

"We don't know," John Wesley said. "One thing I do know, I want to ride strong horses." He sensed that he and his neighbor were about to voice a disagreement, and he didn't want that to happen. The cattle belonged to Josh Bennett, but in his mind he was right about wanting to keep the horses strong. He stood, went to the creek, and washed his plate. "Good stew," he said when he came back. "Man can't ask for anything better."

On the third day one of the Jenkins boys watched them until noon, then disappeared. They also lost Turkey Creek.

"I knew the creek turned south along here," Josh Bennett said. "There's another creek that comes out of the hills up ahead, but we won't git there tonight. We'll have to make a dry camp. Let's let these brutes fill up while we got a chance."

"Thirsty cattle are hard to handle. How far ahead is that other creek?"

"Noon tomorrow. If that feller told me correct, the railroad siding is only about a quarter-mile north of it. I sure hope he told me correct and there is a siding and a pen over there."

"Anybody can go a day and night without water. We'll be all right."

Just the same, both men got little sleep that night. Cattle that had been grazing in the mountains where water was plentiful didn't want to bed down with dry throats. It took both men to keep them together. Though they changed horses during the night, by daylight all four of the horses were tired and slow.

"You was right about campin' early t'other night, John.

Otherwise we'd be afoot by now."

"Let's hope we find that other creek before dark."

"We oughtta come to the railroad by dark, too."

The cattle walked slowly, mouths open, slobbering. The horses were tired and getting more so as the men rode back and forth, yelling, whistling to keep the cattle moving. Cattle that had been wild were now tame enough that the men could ride up to them and slap them with catch ropes. They didn't stop for a noon meal, but kept going. John Wesley had gone without water before, and he knew he'd survive. His only worry now was the horses. Then, about the time the sun sat on the western horizon, the cattle started walking faster, lowing deep in their throats.

Josh Bennett yelled across the herd, "That creek can't be far ahead."

"It's no more than a couple miles," John Wesley yelled back. "The calves smell water."

It was there, running shallow now that only a little snow was left in the mountain crevices. But there was enough water for men and animals. The men rode upstream from the cattle where the water hadn't been muddied, dropped their reins, fell flat on their stomachs and put their faces in the water. Their horses drank beside them.

Thirst sated, Josh sat back on his heels and packed his pipe. "Nothin' man-made ever tasted better." He looked around him, turning his head to look to the north. "Railroad's s'posed to be up there somewhere. Can't see 'er, though."

John Wesley said, "Unless I've got my directions mixed up, it has to be within a mile or so. Rosebud is thirty or thirty-five miles west, on the other side of the mountains."

"She's gotta be there. I hope that feller was right about a siding and a pen."

"We'll find out in the morning. This creek turns east over yonder. I'll bet it runs alongside the railroad for a ways."

There was no wood to build a good fire, only the brown grass, which they pulled up by the handfuls. The grass burned quickly, but put out enough heat to at least partially warm the remainder of the stew. That and stale bread made up their supper. They took turns watching the herd again that night, and at dawn they had to eat half-cooked bacon.

"Tell you what, John, I'll git on my horse and ride north and find the railroad and the siding. Then we'll know which way to go."

"Go ahead. These calves will be happy to hang around the water. They won't be hard to handle."

Josh Bennett was back in two hours. "Found 'er. Right where that feller said. A long siding, a stout pen, and ever'thing. Ever'thing but a rail car."

"Does the creek run near it?"

"About a quarter-mile. Let's move 'em over there." The pen was strong, built by a company that could afford better materials than a rancher could. Iron rails ran east and west, out of sight in both directions. There was more to do.

"Beef on the hoof ain't worth a nickel to a cowman unless he's got a buyer," Josh Bennett said. "I'm gonna have to go to Rosebud and find a buyer, or arrange for a rail car and ship these brutes to Denver. If I'm lucky I'll find a buyer and let him do the shippin'."

"There's good grass around here, Josh. I'll keep them together 'til you get back."

"I'll start first thing in the mornin'."

They held the calves near the creek, and the older man used his saddle horse to drag up an abandoned railroad tie. John Wesley went to work with an axe and soon had a good fire going. Josh opened another gallon lard can full of stew, and both men took a careful smell of it before they declared it fit to eat. Stomach full, John Wesley saddled one of his horses and was ready to take his turn herding cattle. But before he put his foot in the stirrup, his neighbor spoke in a solemn tone:

"Did you see 'em, John?"

"Yeah, I saw 'em."

"Recognize 'em?"

"I don't know. There's three of them."

"Come from the north, but the Jenkinses could of rode far enough around us to stay out of sight."

"They ain't friends."

Josh Bennett couldn't keep the worry out of his voice. "Goddamit, wish I would've hired another man. Two more. We're in a jackpot here, John."

Mounted now, John Wesley said, "There ain't nothing we can do but go on with your plans."

"Yeah, John. But I ain't gonna sleep tonight. You keep your eyes open, too."

Voice grim, John Wesley touched spurs to his horse. "Yeah. I'll do that."

CHAPTER 10

Daylight was a relief. During his turn in the night John Wesley had stayed off his horse as much as he could, and even after his neighbor took over, he didn't sleep. Every time he started to doze off a calf lowed or a horse nickered or a coyote yapped or something, and he was wide awake again, expecting to hear gunshots.

With daylight came hope that everything was peaceful. Still, Josh Bennett was apologetic. "I'm sure sorry to leave you alone like this, John. If you want, I'll stay and you can go to town. You can go to the hotel and look for a buyer. Cattle buyers stay in hotels. Or the railroad depot. If you don't find a buyer you can go to the depot and tell the station master or whatever he's called and arrange for a cattle car. Prob'ly need two cars."

"No, you go. They're your cattle and you know how to sell cattle. Next year you can help me sell a few. Whoever those three riders were they're gone now. Maybe just some cowboys on their way to town."

"You sure, John? The soonest I can get back is tomorrow late."

"Yeah. Go ahead."

Josh Bennett mounted a long-legged sorrel and looked down at John Wesley. "Listen, John, these calves ain't your responsibility. If you think they are I am hereby releasin' you of all responsibilities. That's in case some gunnies come around and drive 'em off. Don't try to fight 'em. Leave. Git. Save your hide. Don't git yourself killed on my account. I'd rather lose the cattle. Understand?"

"Yeah, sure."

"I mean it. I'll try to hire somebody to help gather 'em again. I don't expect one man to keep 'em in a bunch by hisself."

"I'll do the best I can. They're grazing peaceful now. Maybe I can get some Zs."

"If nothin' happens I'll be back tomorrow night for sure." With that, the older man touched spurs to the sorrel and took off at a trot, heading west along the railroad tracks.

"Adios," John Wesley said.

He watched his neighbor ride away, then checked the hobbles on the extra horses and the packhorse. Every now and then he took a good look around, studying the horizon in all directions. He was out of the Turquoise Basin and on a high plateau with another range of mountains about a mile north. The Blue Range was west. It slanted down onto the plateau and leveled off with it. If the railroad ever went to Cloudcroft, here was where it would fork, with one branch on the north side of the Blue Range and another on the south. The creek came out of the mountains to the north, and a few cottonwoods grew along its banks. Only a few. Some tall weeds lined the bank for a short distance.

Riding around the cattle, he saw that the grass had been grazed on earlier that year. About a month earlier, he reckoned. Josh Bennett's cattle wouldn't be the first to be shipped from the railroad pen. Grass was plentiful. The cattle and the hobbled horses were grazing contentedly. He dismounted, loosened the cinches and hobbled the horse. While it cropped the grass he lay back with his hands under his head and stared at the sky. It was blue, not a cloud in sight. The sun was warm on his face. It felt good. He dozed.

After an hour he sat up with a snort, eyes trying to take in everything in all directions. He had a feeling. He didn't know what. Just a feeling that something wasn't right. But the cattle had scattered only a little and the horses were still going after the grass. His saddled horse had moved about fifty yards with its forefeet hobbled, but was grazing, taking one hobbled jump-step at a time, and wasn't trying to go farther.

Stiff and tired, he stood, took another long look around, sat again. In a little while he'd get horseback and go turn the cattle back this way, keep them from wandering too far. Then he'd change horses and see what he could find in the pack panniers to eat.

The loaf of bread had green spots on it, but he pinched them off and ate part of the loaf anyway. He opened an airtight can of dried beef and ate half of that. A tin cup of water from the creek finished his meal. Horseback again, he rode south, got on the other side of the cattle that had drifted south and turned them back, slowly, not trying to hurry. The cattle were well-fed and watered now and wild again. They wouldn't let a man on a horse get too close. He kept his distance.

As always, he was looking around, studying everything in sight. He saw smoke. It was over east. Puffs of smoke, like Indian smoke signals. Black smoke. Then he saw the steam locomotive. Fascinated, he sat his horse and watched it come closer. It seemed to be moving slow at first, but as it got closer he was surprised at how fast it was moving. As fast as a horse could run. Maybe a little faster. The hobbled horses saw it and their heads came up. The cattle saw it too, and moved away from it, away from the tracks.

Uh-oh, John Wesley said under his breath. Don't blow the whistle. For Pete's sake, don't blow the whistle.

Two big steers trotted away, stopped, turned and stared at the engine, turned and trotted farther away. John Wesley loped around them, got on the south of them, slowed his horse to a walk. Cattle were trotting his way.

"Don't do it," he muttered.

The engine was pulling nine rail cars, including one passenger car and a caboose. Faces were pasted to the windows of the passenger car, and when it came closer some of the passengers waved at him. He waved back.

The engine was passing the siding now, big wheels driving, smoke puffing from the smoke stack. Red fire was flashing in the fire box. A man in the cab waved, a man wearing a striped cap and a red bandana around his throat. The cattle were moving, trotting. Four started to run.

"No, don't," John Wesley pleaded. "Don't do it."

The man in the striped cap waved again, reached above his head and pulled a chain. A steam whistle shrieked.

In an instant the cattle were running. Running wild. Running right at John Wesley. He spurred his horse and kept ahead of them, moving to the west, slowed and let the herd leaders pass him, then spurred his horse again and tried to stay abreast of them.

Yelling, cursing, he rode recklessly, trying to turn the leaders, get the herd milling. There was no stopping them. Desperate, he drew the Army Colt and fired a shot in the air, hoping the sound would turn the cattle. It didn't work. They kept running. Running like a herd of deer. Another shot came from somewhere. John Wesley looked back. Three riders. Riding hard, six-guns in their hands, shooting.

"Hey," he yelled, knowing they couldn't hear him.

"Hey, what the hell're you doing?"

Then he knew what they were doing. One man aimed his six-gun at John Wesley. A bullet zinged past his head.

"Hey," he yelled. But that was useless. He spurred his horse on and kept up with the herd leaders. But now the three riders were on the other side of the herd, about two hundred yards away. They were shooting in his direction.

Muttering through his teeth, John Wesley said, "You sons of bitches. You goddam sons of bitches."

His horse was running its best, hooves pounding. Taking aim from the back of a running horse wasn't easy, but John Wesley squinted down the short barrel of the Army Colt, got the nearest man in the sights and squeezed the trigger. The man dropped his pistol and grabbed his right shoulder. He pulled his horse down to a trot.

The other two men fired faster, filling the air with lead. A bullet thudded into the fork of John Wesley's saddle, and he felt the heat from another as it passed near his face. He aimed again, carefully, squeezed the trigger. Nothing happened.

"Dammit," he muttered. "Can't waste shots. Have to aim better."

More shots came his way. They were shooting for his horse. Sure, he muttered, shoot my horse and put me afoot and the cattle are yours. Can't let that happen. The horse was still running hard, but slowing.

"Don't quit on me now," he pleaded. "Keep going, feller."

He aimed again. Carefully. Squeezed the trigger.

The rider he'd fired at slumped in his saddle, fell forward, then leaned back, pulling on the reins to keep from falling. Pulled on the horse's mouth, pulled its head up. Pulled its head up so far the horse stumbled and fell. The rider rolled off, got up and bent low, holding his face in both hands.

That left only one armed rider on the other side of the herd. He was keeping up with the cattle, riding hard. John Wesley grinned. "The odds are even now, you son of a bitch." But he was spurring hard to keep his horse running. The other man's horse seemed to be stronger. The race would soon be over. Unless...

He aimed again, putting the front sight on the man's shoulders. The sight bobbed. He waited, then squeezed the trigger.

The rider pulled his horse to a stop, fired a hasty shot at John Wesley and tried to shoot again. He couldn't—had to reload.

John Wesley kept going, spurring hard. He looked back and grinned again. The rider had turned his horse around. "Don't like the odds now, huh?"

Holstering the Army Colt, he allowed his horse to slow to a lope, then to a trot. The cattle were still running, but they had slowed, too. Now they were scattering. With no riders to keep them together they were scattering in three directions.

He stopped on a rise where he could see clear back to the railroad. The three riders had quit. They were going northwest. Two were hanging onto their saddle horns. One was hanging on with both hands while another led his horse.

John Wesley got down and loosened the cinches. The horse stood spraddle legged, sides heaving.

"Gawd damn," he said aloud. "Those sons of bitches tried to kill me."

He sat on the ground, keeping an eye on the three riders fading fast into the distance, and ejected empty shell casings from the six-gun.

They'd tried to kill him and steal the cattle. If they could shoot better he'd be dead. Or afoot. Which was almost as good as dead. Who the humped up hell were they? Old Man Jenkins and his two sons? Yeah. Three of them. Had to be. What the hell did they hope to do? They couldn't sell the calves without working over the brands, and fresh brands would be easy to see if anyone was looking for them. Maybe they expected to sell the calves one or two at a time to folks in Rosebud. Town people wouldn't care about brands, only the meat. Especially if they could buy beef cheap.

"Gawd damn."

He took .44 cartridges from his gun belt and reloaded the Army Colt. A good gun. He handled it fondly, and remembered trading a horse for it somewhere in west Texas. He was only a kid then, but like all kids he was fascinated by guns, and he'd practiced with the Colt all the time. In one town he'd traded a calf for a hundred rounds of .44 shells, and shot them all up in a few weeks. His favorite game was to shoot at bottles on a fence from the back of a running horse. At first his horses had spooked and tried to buck when he shot from their backs, but he'd always let out a yell to break the quiet and give them some warning before he fired. They'd gotten used to it. Now he shook his head when he realized that that kind of practice had saved his life.

He'd hit two men. Took them right out of the fight, leaving the third one so discouraged he'd given up. Whether the men he'd shot lived or died was something he might never know. Or, well, yeah, if two of the Jenkinses were never seen again, he'd know what became of them. Which of the three did he shoot? Come to think of it he hadn't recognized them. They'd had jacket collars turned up and their hats pulled down. And their clothes were...hell, anybody can change clothes. Their horses were bays, but so were most horses. His horse was a bay.

The horse was getting its wind now, but still had its head down and nostrils flared.

"Take your time, feller," John Wesley said. "When you feel like it we'll go back and get this saddle off so you can rest better. I'll catch one of Josh's horses and do what I can to keep these calves from leaving the country."

He knew it would take at least two days for one man to gather the cattle again, but by dark he had some of them turned back toward the creek. He ate the rest of the tinned beef and the part of the bread that was edible. He didn't build a fire, fearing that the third man might come back in the dark, looking for revenge. When he finished eating, he carried the tarp and blankets into the tall weeds along the creek, rolled up in them and tried to sleep. As tired as he was, sleep didn't come right away. In his mind every rodent that ran through the weeds was a man with a gun, trying to find him. Eventually, he forced his mind to relax and he slept.

He slept with his fingers wrapped around the walnut butt of the Army Colt .44.

CHAPTER 11

After riding all morning and most of the afternoon, he still hadn't found all the cattle. Now he was eight miles south of the railroad and the creek, and he'd counted fifty-six. Pushing a dozen head back north, he didn't see the two riders coming until they'd seen him. Immediately, he looked for a low spot, an arroyo, a draw, anything. There was no place to take cover. Two riders. Coming at a trot. All he could do was stay still and wait. Maybe they were friendly. He waited.

Then he stood in his stirrups and waved his hat. One of the riders was Josh Bennett. Josh had already seen him, and lifted his mount into a lope. The other man followed. Horses blowing from the run, they came up and stopped. John Wesley and his neighbor grinned at each other without speaking for a moment, then the older man said:

"I saw that train go by just before I got to town yesterday, and I was afraid it might've stampeded the calves. And, boy howdy, they're sure scattered to hell and gone."

"That train wasn't the only thing that boogered them," John Wesley said, and he told about the three riders and the gunfire. The older man's eyes narrowed.

"I was afraid somebody'd try to steal some beef on the hoof. You shot two of 'em, you say?"

"Yeah, they were still horseback the last time I saw them, but they were hanging onto everything that stuck out on a saddle."

"Old Man Jenkins and his two offspring?"

"That's my guess, but I didn't see their faces. What do you reckon they tried to do?"

Josh Bennett shifted in his saddle. His horse wanted to reach the grass, but its rider held the reins tight. "Can't b'lieve they'd expect to steal the herd. Too easy to track down. Prob'ly figured to scatter 'em, then pick out two or three head and drive 'em home. That way they could eat good beef all winter without havin' to butcher their own."

The other man was dressed in rancher's clothes, with wool pants tucked inside high-top boots and a grey hat pulled low. He hadn't spoken, only listened. John Wesley looked him over, then looked back at his neighbor.

"I can believe that. I was thinking the same thing."

The other man spoke then, "It happens. A few drifters come along, see a herd of cattle guarded by only one man and figure to get some free beef. Happened over by Durango about a month ago. Fifty head of prime beefs. The sheriff over there and a bunch of cowboys went after them and found most of them, but not all." He grinned. "Some folks over there are feasting on somebody else's beef."

"Josh," Josh Bennett half-turned in his saddle, "meet George Shanks. He's a buyer for a Denver packin' house. We agreed on price per pound, and if we can agree on how many pounds we got here, he's bought hisself some cattle."

The two men nodded at each other. "Well," John Wesley said, "you could fool me. I've never seen cattle weighed."

"I have," the buyer said. "We weigh them all the time at the stockyards. I'm hard to fool."

"How many've you found, John?"

"I counted fifty-six. I haven't been very far east."

Glancing at the western horizon, Josh said, "Well, we've got plenty of time. Won't get a stock car for two days, then we'll have to wait another two days for an engine to pick it up."

"Meantime, these calves're feeding on free grass."

"Speakin' of feed," Josh said, "I brought some fresh chuck back with me. Expect you're feelin' a little hollow."

"I could eat the seams out of a whore's drawers."

Chuckling, Josh Bennett turned his horse around. "Well then, let's push this bunch ahead of us and get back to the creek. I'll do the cookin'.""

It was dark when they got back to their camp, but John Wesley soon had a fire going and got busy chopping more pieces off the abandoned railroad tie. His neighbor soon had steaks frying in a heavy iron skillet and potatoes baking in hot coals. They hobbled all their horses.

"Them calves was glad to git back to water," Josh Bennett allowed. "They won't go far tonight."

They ate until they were stuffed, and the cattle buyer helped wash the dishes in the creek, then grabbed the axe and chopped more firewood. He was a cattleman, John Wesley had seen right from the beginning, and knew how to do his share of the work. John Wesley was ready to hit the blankets as soon as the dishes were washed, but he sat by the fire, blinking and yawning, only half-awake.

"See you slept over in the weeds last night, John. Lucky the rats didn't chaw on you."

"I heard something moving around, but nothing could have kept me awake."

"'Minds me of a big windy I heard over to Cripple Creek." Josh Bennett finished tamping tobacco in his pipe and lit it. "About them big rats on top of Pikes Peak. Ever hear of the Pikes Peak Rats?"

"No," John Wesley said, awake now, expecting a story.

"Me neither," said George Shanks.

"Well, ever'body else has." Josh Bennett blew two puffs of smoke toward the fire. "It was all over New York and England and Germany. Folks came from thousands of miles away to see them rats."

John Wesley waited for his neighbor to go on. George Shanks sensed a story coming and he too waited.

"Feller was a sergeant in the U.S. Army. They sent 'im up on top of that mountain to man a weather station. Took his wife and little girl with 'im. Had a wood-burning stove to keep 'em warm, and had a big battery and a coil of wire for somethin' or other. Never did know what all that stuff was for. Somethin' to do with a telegraph, I reckon."

Two more puffs on the corncob pipe. "Way that feller tells it they woke up one night and found their shack full of rats. Rats as big as skunks. Figgered they come in the window. Had a quarter of ham hangin' from the ceilin' and the rats were chawin' that right down to the bone.

"Well, that feller jumps out of bed and starts to whalin' rats with an Indian war club he'd found somewhere, but there was too many of 'em. They chawed up the meat and went after the sergeant and his wife. He beats on rats 'til he's winded and still they come. While he was whalin' away at 'em he accidentally knocks the stove pipe down and that gives 'im an idee. He puts his feet through them pipes and pulls 'em on like a pair of pants."

He paused, sucked on his pipe, discovered it had gone out, and reached in his shirt pocket for a leather tobacco pouch. Not until he had the pipe loaded and burning again did he go on with his story. John Wesley was wide awake, waiting, knowing his neighbor would take his time.

"Well, that kept 'em off him, but there was his wife and little girl. The woman was jumpin' and hollerin' and stompin' but her legs was gittin' chawed up. Then she gets an idee."

Another pause. George Shanks couldn't stand it. "Yeah? Yeah?"

"Well, she grabs that coil of wire, never mindin' the shock, hooks it up to that battery and throws it across the room. The wire uncoils and squirms around like somethin' alive. Ever' time it touches a rat sparks fly and the rat fries. Once it touched the stove pipe around her husband's legs, and he lets out a whoop and purt-near makes a hole in the roof."

Another pause and Josh Bennett looked at the two men to see if they were listening. Both men were chuckling at the mental image Josh had painted.

"Well, with him knockin' hell out of 'em with that club, and her a stompin' on 'em and that wire a burnin' their asses, the rats give up the battle and pour out through the window. Man and wife was so beat that they forgot about their little girl. When they remembered her it was too late. Wasn't nothin' much left of her."

The two listeners weren't chuckling now. Their faces had turned solemn. Josh Bennett puffed on his pipe and stared into the fire.

"They buried her on the trail about halfway down to Colorado City. Dug a grave the best they could and piled rocks on it. Put up a cross and a board with some words carved on it. I was along there one day looking for some yellow stuff and saw the grave." Josh Bennett's voice had dropped to a low tone now. He talked as if to himself. "I'll never forget the words. Erin, the little girl's name was. The words said..." he paused again, remembering. Then:

> "Fair Cynthia with her starry train
> Shall miss thee in thy silent rest
> And waft one sweet, one spheric strain
> To Erin dear among the blest."

All were silent. The three men stared into the fire, each with his own thoughts. Finally, Josh Bennett beat the dottle out of his pipe on the heel of his boot, put the pipe in his shirt pocket and stood.

"Gents, it's time this old son rested his bones."

With three of them riding, the cattle were rounded by mid-afternoon the next day, and all they could do then was wait for a train. In case the next locomotive engineer who came along was thoughtless enough to blow his whistle, they kept the cattle a mile south of the tracks. Once they were rounded up, haggling over weight began.

George Shanks rode among the calves, looked at each one, rode back to Josh Bennett. "five fifty five."

Shaking his head, Josh said, "Naw. Six hundred easy."

The buyer shook his head, too. "I've seen too many cattle on the scales. Some of these calves'll go five eight-five, and some will weigh no more than five hundred. They'll average five fifty-five."

Pointing, Josh Bennett said, "See that steer over there. The spotted one? How'd you like to rassle him? That booger'll go over six hundred."

"Shovel some grain to him for a couple of weeks and he might, but not now. However, for the sake of an argument, I'll say five seventy."

John Wesley listened. Though he'd never seen cattle weighed he'd seen his uncles guess the weight of livestock, and he'd learned what to look for. In his estimation, the cattle would average around five hundred and eighty pounds. But he kept quiet.

"Five eighty-five," Josh Bennett said.

The buyer appeared to be thinking about it. He rode through the cattle again, came back, looked at the horizon, at John Wesley and at Josh Bennett. "Five seventy-four and that's final."

"Lest's do some cal-clatin' here," Josh Bennett said. "I figgered on gettin' at least twenty six bucks per head. How's that?"

"Five seventy-five and that's final."

"There are other packin' houses."

"Find another buyer, then. Or ship 'em yourself."

"Five eighty."

"All right, I'll split the difference. Five seventy-seven. When I went to school that'd come to right at twenty-six per head. That's figuring four and a half cents per pound, and that's what we settled on."

"Agreed."

"Soon's we get 'em loaded I'll make out a check. You can cash it at any bank."

After that, men and horses got some badly needed rest.

Spotting a stock car in front of the loading chute was no simple matter. The train had to drop off the way car before it pulled onto the siding. With a brakeman waving directions, the engineer positioned one of two stock cars, pulled ahead of the siding and backed up to the way car again. He had to lean far out of his cab to see the brakeman's signals.

Passengers in the one Pullman car watched with interest. One gent with muttonchop whiskers and a derby hat stood on the car platform and yelled, "What's this for, mister?"

"Cattle," Josh Bennett yelled back.

"I don't see any cattle."

"You won't 'til we're ready to load 'em."

The train jerked then and the passenger had to grab an iron railing to keep from being thrown off. Long-handled rail switches were thrown and locked with big padlocks, and the train pulled away, puffing smoke and jerking rail cars, toward the town of Rosebud. Two cattle cars sat on the siding in front of the pen.

Another day and a half of waiting and the train came back. The cattlemen were expecting it and had the calves corralled. While the train dropped off the way car, they opened the door of the first stock car and with yells and whirling lariats herded calves up the loading chute. They waited for the engineer and brakeman to position the second car, then loaded the rest of the cattle.

"Couldn't hold many more," Josh Bennett said when they'd slammed the car door shut and latched it.

"These cars will carry forty head of grown stuff," George Shanks said. "Saw the horns off of 'em and you can get more in it."

Their work done, the buyer wrote out a bank draft for one thousand nine hundred and seventy-three dollars and handed it to Josh Bennett. The rancher read it carefully, folded it and put it in his pocket. After shaking hands all around, George Shanks got on his horse and rode away toward Rosebud.

"Well, John, wanta start for home now or wait 'til mornin'?"

"Let's get started and see how far we can go before dark."

It took two days to get back, and when they rode through Jenkins country they kept their eyes turned to the northern horizon. Nothing human was seen, and Josh allowed, "Reckon you whipped the shit out of 'em, John. They ain't likely to be lookin' for another fight."

"No, not out in the open. But the one that wasn't hit might be wanting revenge."

"Keep your eyes peeled."

At John Wesley's cabin, late in the afternoon, Josh Bennett said, "I'll deposit this check in my account in Cloudcroft, John, and in a week or so I can draw some cash off of it and I'll pay you for your help. If you need anything before then, come on over and we'll find somethin'."

"I can last a week or more. Right now I've got to hunt up my horses and count my cattle. Want to come in for a cup of coffee?"

"Naw. Thanks just the same. If I keep goin' I can git home before dark."

"See you soon, then." John Wesley watched his neighbor ride on, leading two horses. He put his two horses in the corral and threw some hay to them. "This is one of those times when I'm gonna have to feed you," he said to the horses. Then he went to his cabin.

A gray packrat ran down the far wall and disappeared through a crack between two logs when he opened the door, but nothing had been disturbed. There was something out of place on the table, though. A scrap of paper. No, a sheet of paper. He picked it up, carried it to the door where the light was better. A note. Written in a neat feminine hand.

> *Mr. Budeen.*
>
> *I'm sorry you weren't at home. Please forgive me for coming into your house uninvited. I have something I want to talk to you about. It is something which I believe will interest you. Please come to see me at your earliest convenience. I am staying at the hotel in Cloudcroft.*
>
> > *Sincerely,*
> > *Valerie Mitchell.*

CHAPTER 12

He couldn't just drop everything and ride off to town. He had work to do. But he would go to town as soon as he could. That pretty young woman wanted to see him and he couldn't imagine why. It was something to think about. It was on his mind constantly for two days. Then he saw something else to think about.

One of his calves was dead. One of the biggest ones. He found the remains in the pine hills three miles north of his homestead. Paw tracks were all around it. Not bear tracks. A cougar.

Anger swept through John Wesley. His body burned with anger. The calf was an economic loss, and he couldn't afford to lose. Damn it.

Most of the calf had been eaten, but there was a meal or two left for a big cat. Maybe the son of a bitch would come back. A calf-killing cat could put a small rancher out of business in a hurry. I've got to get the son of a bitch, John Wesley said to himself. He swore silently, then out loud.

"This cow business ain't what it's cracked up to be. If the goddam blizzards don't kill off your stock, the droughts will. Or the thieves. Or the goddam cougars. Always something. They call this free land. Free, hell. Anything a man makes off it he earns two or three times over. What chance has a man got?"

No use standing there cussing. He'd come back that night with a rifle. Tie his horse to a tree and sit there and wait in the dark and hope for a shot at the calf-killing son of a bitch.

* * *

It was a long night. Long and cold. This late in the year the nights were colder than a witch's tit. Huddled inside his plaid mackinaw, John Wesley sat under a tree and waited. His horse stamped its feet impatiently. That and the wind sighing through the tree tops were the only sounds. He waited, rifle across his lap, trying to see in the dark. Nothing showed up. Probably because of the horse. The cat saw the horse and knew something wasn't right. John Wesley would have to leave the horse at home and walk up here.

At daylight, standing stiffly, trying to get the blood circulating through his legs again, he decided he'd do that. Walk back up here and spend another night under this goddam tree. The cat might smell him, and it would all be for nothing, but what the hell else could a man do? It was even colder the second night. A full moon shone through the treetops. The treetops swayed in the night wind, causing the moon to blink at him. He sat cross-legged until his knees ached, then straightened his legs, slowly, quietly. He wanted to stand and stamp his feet and wave his arms to get warm, but didn't dare. The night wore on. He'd slept a little in his cabin that day, but not much. Now, in spite of the cold, he was fighting to stay awake. He was numb with cold.

Daylight was coming. The trees were taking shape. The dead calf, what was left of it, was still there. The cat wasn't going to show. He might as well go back to the cabin and get warm.

Something moved. Over there in the shadows. Or was it his imagination?

No. Something was over there.

Eyes straining he watched. Yeah. Something was coming. His fingers on the rifle tightened.

Aw dammit. A coyote.

Disappointment swept through him, made him remember how cold he was. The coyote didn't kill that calf. Coyotes didn't kill cattle, except newborn ones, and only then when the cow was too weak to get up and fight. This one had smelled the meat and was coming to help himself. It approached cautiously, then tore into the dead calf, pulling with its teeth, gulping down meat without chewing.

Suddenly it jumped up and ran. John Wesley stayed still and watched, wondering why. Then he knew.

His heart beat faster, and his hands on the rifle trembled. The cougar.

It came out of the shadows, stopped, stood still, then padded on. Its long tail almost dragged the ground. Its tawny head moved slowly from side to side, looking. It stopped again. Did it smell him?

He wanted to bring the rifle up and aim, but the cat would see movement and take off into the dark shadows. He had to bring the rifle up. Afraid to breathe, he slowly raised the gun, got it hip high, cocked the hammer back.

Crouching now, the cougar looked his way, crawled slowly, belly to the ground. John Wesley was still sitting, wishing he were standing, carefully raising the rifle to his shoulder.

The cat jumped. Sprang right at him. Arcing in the air, a good six feet off the ground. Mouth wide open, long fangs bared.

John Wesley fired without putting the gun to his shoulder, fired as the big cat arced above him. He fell flat as the cat hit him and felt the wind knocked from his lungs. He thought he was about to be killed.

For a few seconds he was only half-conscious. The world was spinning, shapeless. Then gradually his lungs resumed pumping and his vision steadied. He was alive. The cat was on top of him, but not moving. He struggled to get up. The cat was heavy. His hands were still on the gun, and he let go of it and shoved upward with both hands, rolling the dead animal off him.

He got to his knees and, trembling, he stood, knees aching. Dragging the sleeve of his mackinaw across his eyes, he looked down at the cougar. Its mouth was open in death. Gawd, it was a big son of a bitch. At least seven feet long. It had claws that could cut like a bunch of knives, and teeth that could rip the flesh off an elephant. The calf never had a chance. Hell, a horse would be lucky to get away from this brute.

Whew. With knees sore from sitting too long on the ground, he squatted and picked up the rifle. He leaned against the tree and tried to get his thoughts together. Ought to skin it. Nobody would believe how big it was if he didn't have a hide to show.

He walked around in a circle to get the stiffness out of his body, then lifted his skinning knife out of its belt holster. One of the things the rawhiders were good at was skinning animals and tanning hides. It was something they all had to learn at an early age. John Wesley had the cougar skinned in about forty minutes. He cut off the head and peeled as much hide and flesh off the skull as he could, then wrapped it up in the hide.

He walked home, carrying the rifle in one hand and holding the rolled up hide on his shoulder with the other. It was heavy, and it was a long walk home.

After he got there it took an hour to scrape all the flesh off the cougar skin, rub the animal's brains into it, and nail it to an outside wall, stretched tight. When it dried he'd take it inside and use it for a rug or to keep the winter wind from blowing through some of the cracks between the logs. Grinning, he said, "Old Josh won't believe the size of this son of a bitch 'til I show him the hide."

He realized he was talking to himself again.

There was no sharp dividing line between his range and the Jenkinses'. There was no line at all. The Jenkinses always drove his cattle west when they drifted too far in their direction, but he'd never bothered their cattle. When he thought about it he had to admit that they were there first and had a right to be there. But now he rode east in the high timbered hills looking for eight of his cows that he hadn't found. The farther he rode, the more the hair on the back of his neck rose. He carried both his guns and was ready to drop off his horse and hit the ground at the slightest warning.

Cow tracks and droppings told him he was getting close to someone's cattle. The tracks didn't tell him whose. When he found them, he saw his cows were mixed with nine others carrying the Broken O brand. Reining up, he took a long look around. The cattle were grazing at the bottom of a grassy hill. A thin stream ran between the cattle and the edge of a forest of spruce and pine.

If he was being watched, he was being watched from the woods. But, naw, they wouldn't be back in the timber waiting for him. Hell, they had their own work to do. Besides, unless they healed fast, there was only one of them able to fork a horse.

Just the same, the hair on the back of his neck tingled until he had his cows cut out and headed west. He didn't yell at the cows nor make any more noise than he had to.

By dark he knew where all his cattle were. He'd lost only one. And when he thought about it he figured he was lucky. The rawhiders had always watched their cattle and seldom lost any, but up here where he didn't see his cattle for months at a time during the summer he was lucky to lose only one. In fact, he was damned lucky. There were too many ways for cattle to die. There were the poisonous flowers called Larkspur that were sure death for cattle. Another problem was porcupines. Three times during the summer he'd had to rope calves, tie them down, and pull porcupine quills out of their noses. If he hadn't found them, they would have starved. No animal could eat with a nose full of porcupine quills.

Damned porcupines. The calves hadn't meant them any harm, just wanted to smell the strange little creatures. Damned porcupines had to slap them in the noses with their tails. Without human help the calves would have died a slow, agonizing death. Cattlemen hated porcupines.

Yep, this cattleman had been lucky. Now to get them through the winter and the calving. Cows sometimes died giving birth. A cowman had to be always on horseback, ready to play midwife. It was a bloody, dirty job, but the calves meant money in the bank.

It was one problem after another, but John Wesley knew cattle and horses, and liked working with them. A man had to do something to earn a living.

In fact, that night, after a bath out of a bucket, lying in his bed covered with warm blankets, hot coals still popping in the stove, he decided he was mostly satisfied with his life. He'd collect his pay from Josh Bennett and lay in enough groceries to last the winter. It wasn't a bad life. Except for the loneliness.

The rawhiders traveled in a caravan and were never alone. He didn't like the loneliness. That brought his mind back to the blond young woman named Valerie Mitchell. Now there was a woman. The winters wouldn't be so bad if a man had a woman like that. He could spare a couple of days now. Tomorrow he'd go see her.

CHAPTER 13

Josh Bennett wasn't at home. He was probably up in the hills somewhere horseback. Or maybe he was in town, cashing the check from the cattle buyer. John Wesley went on, getting into Cloudcroft shortly before noon. He rode up and down the four-block main street, looking for his neighbor or a horse belonging to him. He dismounted and looked inside the Toltec Mercantile. Not there.

Instead of eating in the Ponderosa Eatery, he hobbled his horse on the edge of town and ate the sandwich he'd brought. Eating in a café cost money. After he ate, he walked the three blocks down a dirt street to the Cloudcroft Hotel. There were no sidewalks in Cloudcroft, only hitchrails in front of the stores and the saloon. The hotel had a small wooden porch and a step leading up to it. John Wesley stepped onto the porch and looked down at himself. His denim pants and his cotton shirt were wrinkled but clean. He'd washed them in a tub with a scrub board. His boots were scuffed and colorless. Couldn't do anything about that. His face was fresh-shaved, but he needed a haircut. There was no barber in town, and Josh Bennett had been cutting his hair every couple of months.

A man like him had no business calling on a pretty, well-groomed young woman, but hell, she'd asked him to. He opened a wide door and stepped inside.

The lobby took in about fifty square feet. A worn carpet with a flower design covered most of the floor. A few wooden chairs sat along one wall, and a desk was placed against the far wall. Wooden stairs led to the second floor. John Wesley approached the desk hesitantly, fearing he looked out of place. The clerk, a middle-aged bald man wearing wire-rimmed glasses and a shirt with no collar, looked up, and frowned.

"Uh," John Wesley began, "is Miss, uh, Valerie Mitchell in?"

The clerk said nothing, only shook his head. "She ain't? I mean, she's not?"

"Nope."

"Well, uh, is she still staying here?"

"Yep."

"Well, uh, do you think she'll be back pretty soon?"

"Nope."

John Wesley stood in front of the desk, trying to figure out what to say next. And then he began to get angry. This yahoo didn't have to be so damned uppity. Finally, he said, rancor in his voice, "Would you mind too much telling me what the deal is here?"

"She's gone, but I think she'll be back."

"Yeah?" John Wesley was standing with his hands on his hips now, staring hard at the clerk.

"Left on the southbound stage yesterday. Paid a week's rent before she left. Said she'd be back."

"Did she leave anything in her room?"

"Yep. Left some clothes. Took only a little satchel with her."

"Did she say where she was going?"

"Nope. I didn't ask. Wasn't none of my business." Frowning at the floor now, John Wesley pulled at his chin, then looked up. "I apologize for asking so many questions, but she asked me to come see her. Did she have any visitors?"

"One. A man. He stayed here two days and left. He didn't stay in her room. We don't allow that."

"A man. Uh, what did he look like? I mean, a laboring man or what?"

"Good dresser. Looked like a drummer or a businessman."

"Young?"

"'Bout your age."

"Well." He was puzzled, but he didn't know what else to ask about. "Uh, when she comes back would you tell her that John

Wesley Budeen was here to see her? She asked me to come see her."

Picking up a pencil and positioning a sheet of paper on the desk, the clerk prepared to write. "How do you spell Budeen?"

John Wesley spelled it for him and watched him write it down. "Thanks. I appreciate it."

Outside on the dirt street, John Wesley began walking toward the bank, still hoping to see his neighbor. He could use some groceries. He could use a cold beer, too. He would have to buy some groceries pretty soon or live like an Indian. Too bad Josh wasn't at home or here in town. A man ought to have a drink of whiskey or a beer when he came to town.

The Merchants State Bank was a stone building with a wooden floor, two tellers' cages protected by wrought iron, and a big iron safe against a far wall. There were customers in the lobby, but Josh Bennett wasn't among them.

Nothing to do but go home. He was disappointed. First because he hadn't found his neighbor and collected his pay, and second because the pretty blond young woman was out of town. He'd made a trip for nothing. Well, maybe Josh would be at home when he went by on his way back. He was going to have to find him soon. He needed the money.

The first thing he noticed about the young man walking toward him was the hard, mean look on his face. The mean look was directed at John Wesley. The second thing he noticed was the six-gun carried in a cut-away holster low on his right hip, low for a fast draw. The third was that the man was a Jenkins.

He was the younger of the Jenkins boys. No other Jenkins was in sight.

John Wesley tried to walk on past him, pretend he didn't recognize him. It didn't work.

"Hey, squatter."

He turned. Jenkins stood beside a hitchrail on one side of the street. He was standing spraddle-legged, facing John Wesley.

"Yeah?" John Wesley had to stop and face him. He didn't like being called a squatter, but decided not to make anything of it.

"Saw you moving a herd across our country."

"It's a free country."

"We ought to make you pay a toll or somethin'. Your cattle ate some of our grass."

What did he mean *We?* John Wesley wondered. He was the only Jenkins around. The other two were nursing bullet wounds. Was this kid looking for a chance to get even? He thought about saying something sarcastic, like, Did you think you'd take a few calves in payment? But instead, he said:

"It was the only way to the railroad."

"It was our grass. We been savin' it for the winter." He could put the blame on his neighbor. It was Josh Bennett's herd. No, he was the one being challenged. "Well, if you think I'm gonna shell out some money, you're touched in the head."

The kid's hand hovered over his six-gun. "I can take it away from you."

At that, John Wesley had to snort out loud. Did this dumb gunsel think he had any money? Didn't he know the herd belonged to Josh Bennett? Or did he think he'd been paid for his help and would have a few bucks in his pocket?

"Huh," he snorted again. He was glad he'd carried the Army Colt to town with him. But he wished he'd tied it low instead of high on his hip for comfort. In a fast-draw contest, the Jenkins boy might win. Just the same, he'd be damned if he'd back down. He flexed his fingers, and tried to mentally prepare himself for a fast draw—for death.

He watched Jenkins's eyes, tried to read them. The kid knew now that he couldn't run a bluff. One of the two had to back down or draw and shoot. The kid's eyes shifted. He was looking for someone to intervene. He was afraid.

Two men in cattlemen's clothes saw what was happening and stopped to watch. A woman in a long gray dress and a sunbonnet stopped, and held her hand to her mouth.

Young Jenkins's eyes shifted to the left. He wanted out of this. John Wesley had an urge to sneer and say something like, What did you expect, Button? Did you think you could scare me into begging for my life? Didn't your pa teach you any better than that? He thought it over and decided to let the kid save face.

"Listen, Jenkins, we moved that herd as fast as we could, and we didn't use up any more of your grass than we had to. There wasn't any other way." He saw relief in the young man's eyes.

"Well, just don't make a habit of it." Jenkins turned and walked stiff-legged down the street. John Wesley could have yelled something at him like, We'll cross your country any time we need to. But he didn't. He was relieved, too. He'd already shot two of the Jenkinses and he didn't want to shoot the other one. In fact, he didn't want to shoot anybody.

And he sure as hell didn't want to get shot.

"Budeen?"

It was one of the ranchers talking. John Wesley recognized him as a man he'd met in the Uptown Saloon. The rancher was smiling.

"Looked like you two was headed for pistol city. Glad to see you didn't back down. Them Jenkinses are bad medicine."

Grinning crookedly, John Wesley drawled. "I'm not so sure I could beat him."

"But you was ready to try."

"Only if I had to." He considered telling the rancher about trading shots with the Jenkinses twice before, but decided not to.

"Come on in the bar with me and let's have a shot of whiskey."

He wanted to. He could have used a drink of whiskey and a man to bat the breeze with, but if he did he'd be expected to buy the second round. He didn't have the price.

"Thanks, but I've got to get home. Thanks anyway. Some other time."

The weather had been dry and clear, but now it was threatening to snow. John Wesley wanted to keep his cows and calves in the high country as long as he could, but he reckoned it would soon be time to bring them down. The trick was, he reckoned, to keep them on the mountain grass as long as he could without getting them snowed in. The first good snow usually melted before the hard part of winter set in, but it was a warning to stockmen, hunters, and everyone that they had better head for lower elevations. It looked as though the first real storm was about to start.

He was horseback, locating his cattle so he would know where to find them when the time came. He found some of Josh Bennett's JB connected cows and pushed them west with his own. Fresh tracks told him some of the cattle had drifted east. He followed the tracks.

On the top of a high, rocky ridge he reined up and looked across a narrow valley to another boulder-covered ridge. The grass was brown, but plentiful down there. A dozen or more deer grazed. In a few weeks this would be a good place to hunt elk. That is, if the snow allowed him in. Suddenly, his eyes narrowed.

There was a horse down there. A saddled horse. Where was the rider? He scanned the scenery and saw nothing human. The horse was a stocking-legged sorrel, like one of Josh Bennett's. Then he saw the big black and white birds, the magpies.

"Oh no," he groaned as he touched spurs to his mount and rode at a gallop down off the ridge.

The hill was steep and rocky, and the horse slid in places, but John Wesley kept spurring, riding hard.

Magpies were carrion eaters.

When he got closer he could see it was a man lying in the tall grass. John Wesley rode up fast and stepped off before the horse came to a stop. He groaned again, and felt a sick lump rise to his throat.

It was his friend and neighbor, Josh Bennett.

CHAPTER 14

Murder. No doubt about it. The shot had hit Josh in the back, left side, and tore through the heart. There was very little blood. The heart had stopped instantly. Rigor mortis was setting in and the limbs were beginning to stiffen. Shot late yesterday. The cold temperature would keep rigor mortis away longer. That's what John Wesley remembered hearing a lawman say once when he examined the body of a rawhider who had died of natural causes. Sheriff Watkins would want to examine this body where it had fallen, and search the ground for tracks, an empty shell casing, any kind of clue.

But it would be mid-afternoon next day before the sheriff could get up here, and John Wesley wasn't about to let his friend's body lie here overnight for the magpies and coyotes to feed on. Besides, it was spitting snow now, and everything would soon be covered.

With that sick, choking lump in his throat, he brought up the sorrel horse and got the body lying across the saddle, head on one side and feet on the other. He used Josh's catch rope to lash the body on. Josh's hat was left behind as a marker.

"Hell of a way to treat a man, even a dead man," he muttered as he mounted his horse, picked up the sorrel's reins, and headed west.

A horse's back had more motion going downhill than uphill, and John Wesley had to look at the body now and then to make sure it was still in place. The lump in his throat grew bigger. Josh's gray hair was hanging straight down and his face was against a stirrup fender.

"Oh gawd," he groaned.

It was dark when he got to the JB Ranch. The house was unlocked, and he carried his friend's body inside and laid it on the bed. Josh's eyes were open, seeing nothing. He covered the body with a blanket, then went out and got on his horse again. The snow was coming down heavier, and the ground was mostly covered. It would be another night without sleep.

The only business open in Cloudcroft was the saloon. He didn't want to go in there. He didn't want to talk to anybody. But he had to ask where Sheriff Watkins lived. The bartender told him and asked, "Why? Somebody shot or somethin'?"

"Uh," John Wesley said. "Tell you later."

His horse was tired and showing it when he found the sheriff's house. It was a three-room frame house with a log corral and stable in back. He could barely make out the corral and stable in the dark. The house was dark, but a lamp was lit within seconds after he knocked on the door. Sheriff Joseph Watkins opened the door in his sock feet, shirt unbuttoned, holding a lighted lantern. He held the lantern up so it illuminated John Wesley's face.

"Budeen? What in tarnation...?"

"Josh Bennett's been shot, Sheriff. He's dead."

Paunchy Sheriff Watkins cussed the snow and allowed he wished he could have seen the body before it was moved, but he didn't criticize John Wesley for moving it. He asked a lot of questions, such as exactly where and how the body lay, any blood on the ground, any shell casings, how far away the dead man's horse was, and did John Wesley search the ground for tracks? Finally, he got back on his horse.

"Any idea, Budeen?"

"It wasn't robbery. His horse and saddle were here. You've heard, haven't you, about how the Jenkinses get fighting mad every time they see somebody else's cattle over this way?"

"You think it was the Jenkinses?"

"It would be easy to believe, wouldn't it?"

"Yeah, it'd be easy to believe. But right now it would be damned hard to prove."

"Being a man of law you have to have proof."

"You betcha." Sheriff Watkins stared at John Wesley from under his wide hat brim. "And don't you get any ideas about gettin' revenge for your neighbor's murder. You ain't got no proof either."

"What are you gonna do about it?"

The sheriff gave it some thought before answering, "I'll go have a talk with Old Man Jenkins. That's all I can do. But not today. Right now I've got to go to town and get a wagon and move the body to town. Wish we had an undertaker. Have to lay him out in the shed behind my house. Then have to try to find the next of kin. What about his stock? Can you take care of 'em 'til we find an heir? He was your friend."

"Sure. I'll do it. His wife died, but he had a daughter somewhere. A little girl. Living with an aunt, somewhere. You can probably find some letters or something with her name and everything."

They were riding back toward town now, letting their horses take it slow. Snow covered the trail and the rocks, and the horses couldn't see where they were putting their feet down. In places, the footing was treacherous.

"When the judge comes to town I'll get him to appoint somebody to look after Josh's property 'til an heir is found and the place can be sold. I'll have to leave it up to you to watch things until then."

"Yeah, but if you see me riding some of Josh's horses, don't think I'm trying to steal them. I haven't got enough horses to do all the riding I'll have to do."

"I'll remember that."

The sky cleared that afternoon and the sun came out. Still, a cold wind blew down from the hills, and John Wesley reckoned it was time to wash his longhandled underwear. As he rode one of Josh Bennett's horses back to his homestead, his emotions were a mixture of sadness, anger, and frustration.

Old Josh was dead. John Wesley knew he had lost something that could never be replaced. Josh the storyteller, the checker player, the best friend he ever had.

Murdered. Shot in the back.

Damned Jenkinses. Goddam them to hell. Nothing but trouble. Always threatening. Tried twice to kill him. Now they killed Old Josh.

The anger rose in him until it took over his whole body. Every muscle was tense. Kill them. Go over there and wait outside their door and shoot them down as they come out, the way they tried to shoot him. Kill the sons of bitches. Do it. Don't wait for the law. Do your duty as a friend.

Then what? Be arrested for murder himself? That's what the law would do. The sheriff wasn't going to arrest the Jenkinses because he had no proof, but he'd arrest John Wesley. He'd know who shot the Jenkinses. Maybe, if the trial was held in Cloudcroft, he'd be found not guilty. Everyone knew what kind of men the Jenkinses were. Everyone would at least suspect it was the Jenkinses who killed Josh Bennett. They wouldn't convict the man who shot the Jenkinses.

Would they?

"Huh," John Wesley snorted aloud. Who knows what a jury will do. Get some of those Bible thumpers on the jury and they'll convict anybody that doesn't go to their church.

We can't allow any man to take the law into his own hands. That's what the prosecutor would say. No man is above the law. Sure. Then how in hell can the Jenkinses shoot Josh Bennett in the back and get away with it?

Riding on, getting close to home, John Wesley reached a decision. He'd leave it up to the law to take care of the Jenkinses. But from now on he'd carry the Army Colt tied low, and if any Jenkins even looked cross at him, one of them would die.

And the way he felt right now, the sooner the better.

His work had doubled. He was pushing cattle down from the hills now, getting his cattle and Josh Bennett's mixed. Had it not been for Josh Bennett's horses, he couldn't have done it. Twice, he'd spent the night in the JB ranch house.

Both times, he had an urge to open the drawers of the dresser in the bedroom and try to find letters from his neighbor's sister, to learn more about the Bennett family. He was fascinated by that picture on the dresser. But he kept his hands off. He did help himself to Josh's groceries. He was entitled to that much. In fact he was entitled to more than that. Josh was killed before he'd gotten around to paying John Wesley, and now John Wesley had no money to buy groceries for himself. In fact, if he hadn't been able to stay in the JB ranch house, he'd be getting hungry about now.

Let the cattle mix. If he was going to take care of both outfits, he had no choice but to let them mix. They could be sorted in the spring. But if he saw any Broken O cattle, he'd drive them east, out of that territory. And if any Jenkins didn't like it, well, they'd just have to shoot it out.

That was what he was thinking when he rode back to his own cabin around noon and saw a strange horse tied there.

Dismounting, he left his horse on the opposite side of the corrals, where the Jenkins bunch had once left theirs, and stayed behind a big corral post.

"Hey," he yelled. "Hey, you in the house. Come out." She came out immediately, looking a little scared, as if she'd been caught doing something she shouldn't have. When she saw John Wesley she smiled, hesitantly at first, then wider. "Mr. Budeen. You scared me. I was afraid it was someone else out here."

All he could do was stare. He came out from behind the fence post and stared. She was wearing a divided riding skirt with a man's floppy black hat on her blond head. The horse was saddled with a man's saddle.

"I'm sorry," she said. "I didn't mean to invade your privacy. I would like to talk to you, and as usual you weren't at home. I thought I'd leave another note."

"Why, uh..." That was all he could say.

"I'm sorry, too, I wasn't in town when you went looking for me. If I'd known when you were coming I would have been there."

Gawd she was pretty. A pretty woman like her made him realize how much he missed women. For two seconds, he tried to picture her as a homesteader's wife.

"May I talk with you, Mr. Budeen?"

"Why, uh, sure." He walked over to her. "Come in. It's not a fit place for a young lady, but it's all I've got."

"It's a nice cabin. Very masculine, but comfortable-looking."

That mental picture of her as a wife flashed through his mind again as he opened the door. She stepped in. "Have a seat," he said, nodding at a homemade chair held together with rawhide. She sat primly, with her knees together. She wore riding boots.

"Care for some coffee?" He reached for his sack of coffee on the shelf and saw that someone had moved it. Her?

"Thank you, no."

"Can I offer you some dinner? Lunch, I mean. That is if you can eat buckskin steak."

"Pardon me, eat what?"

"Deer meat. Venison. That's all I've got now. Got to get to town and lay in some groceries."

"Yes, you do, don't you."

And he knew from the direct way she said it that she had checked his coffee supply and no telling what else. He glanced at her, puzzled.

"You're out of groceries and out of money, aren't you?" It was an accusation. Now she was no sweet young lady. She was talking like a horse trader or a merchant. "You're flat broke, aren't you, Mr. Budeen?"

"What?" For a moment he was flabbergasted at the change. "Well, uh, yes." He wanted to ask what business it was of hers, but he didn't. He waited, hoping she would say what she'd come here to say.

Valerie Mitchell crossed her legs, leaned back in the chair and pushed the floppy hat back on her blond head. "You worked for Josh Bennett and he owed you some money. He was killed before he could pay you, and that leaves you in a bad way financially."

"How do you know all that?"

"Everyone knows you helped Mr. Bennett drive some cattle to market, and I have a friend at the bank. He hasn't drawn a penny from the check he was given for the cattle. Mr. Budeen, I have a proposition for you."

Dumbfounded and a little irritated, all he could do was frown at her.

103

She went on, "Are you interested?"

"In what?"

"In making some money. A lot of money."

Now he had an inkling of why she was here. And he was curious. "How?"

"It's illegal."

"Huh-uh." He shook his head.

Her eyebrows went up. "Does something illegal scare you? That's hard to believe, Mr. Budeen. You were a rawhider, and the rawhiders had a reputation for working outside the law now and then."

He felt his face getting warm as he stood with his hands on his hips. "What do you know about rawhiders?"

Her mouth curved into a half-smile now. "I've heard."

They stared at each other, John Wesley frowning and Valerie Mitchell half-smiling. Then she said, "Come now, Johnnie. May I call you Johnnie? You're on the verge of failure here. Your only resource is your cattle, and if you are forced to sell cattle to buy groceries your cattle business won't grow. You don't want to do that, do you?"

"What do you know about the cattle business?"

Ignoring the question, she asked another, "What do you say, Johnnie? Are you interested? You certainly can use the money."

He faced her, hands on hips, and suddenly he forced himself to relax. He sat down in a chair across the table from her. "Do what?"

The half-smile grew. "No killing. Nothing like that. It's easy."

"What?" he repeated.

"Rob someone. Someone who is about to rob you."

CHAPTER 15

Now he was thoroughly dumbfounded, and he didn't appreciate her knowing so much about him. But he was also curious. She had gone to some trouble to learn about him. Why? And who was this someone about to rob him? He ran it all through his mind before he asked the obvious question:

"Who?"

The half-smile slowly vanished. "Have you ever heard of the Earl of Ravenshire?"

His frown deepened. "Who the hell is the Earl of Ravenshire? Sounds like a Britisher."

"He is. A very rich Britisher." The half-smile was back. "It's obvious you haven't heard of him. Few people in Colorado have. But you can be sure he will have an effect on the lives of everyone around here."

"How?"

"Have you noticed some strange things going on, Johnnie?"

"Like what?"

"Oh." She cocked her head to one side and pretended to be thinking. "Like some cabins that were started and never completed. Things like that."

He knew immediately what she was talking about: four logs laid out in a square, two small log structures in the high hills which Josh Bennett said might be bear traps. "Yeah? What's that got to do with anything?"

"You homesteaded your property here, Johnnie, and you know how far it is to the nearest U.S. Government land office."

"Sure. Over at Rosebud."

"And that's a long way by wagon or stage."

Nodding, he agreed, "Yeah."

"But not so far on horseback over the Blue Range as you call these mountains."

"Yeah?"

"That is significant, as you will soon discover."

Again, all he could say was, "Yeah?"

"And there are more clues."

"What?"

Sitting up straight, she uncrossed her legs and let the smile slip. "I don't think I should tell you any more right now, Johnnie. Not until I get some kind of promise from you."

Not knowing what to say to that, he said nothing. "You're not ready to commit yourself, are you?"

"Huh-uh. No. I'd sure like to know more about all this, but I'm not gonna rob anybody."

"I think you'll change your mind after you've thought it over." She stood, tall and shapely in her divided riding skirt and blue, lacy blouse. "I'll go now. I'll be at the hotel."

His curiosity was growing by the second. "Uh, Miss Mitchell, does anybody else know what you know?"

"Yes. But very few. And not in this basin. The Earl has people working for him. They are bound to secrecy."

"How did you find out?"

Turning, she said over her shoulder, "That's another bit of information I'm not yet ready to divulge." She went through the door and out to her horse. He followed and started to help her get mounted, but she didn't need any help. Just before she turned the horse around and rode away, she said, "Come see me anytime, Johnnie."

He watched her leave, stood in one spot and watched until she was out of sight. Then he turned and went back inside, muttering to himself, "What the humped-up hell was she talking about. What's going on around here? Pieces of cabins. The land agent three day's travel away. Only one long day on horseback, but a government agent wasn't about to get on a horse. What, what?"

It came to him. Suddenly. Sure, that was it. There was talk in the saloon one night about homesteaders claiming land in the south end of Turquoise Basin, picking spots where there was no water. There were cabins started and not finished. The land agent was far away. It wasn't hard to figure out, now that she'd got him to thinking about it.

Those homesteaders, the men who'd put a few sticks together, weren't really planning to live there. They were just pretending to make some improvements on the land, build something just so they could say they did, knowing the land agent couldn't check on every claim.

Why would they do that? Because somebody was paying them to do it. They were being paid to gain titles and turn the titles over to somebody.

"Huh," John Wesley smarted aloud. "Somebody called the Earl of Ravenshire. That gentleman, whoever the hell he is, wants this whole basin, and he's scheming to get it cheap.

"Well, he, by God, ain't gonna get mine. He ain't gonna get Josh Bennett's. And the Jenkinses...huh." John Wesley chuckled. "Wait 'til the son of a bitch tries to take something away from Old Man Jenkins and his two gun-toting sons. Those three would fight the whole Union Army.

"That is, if they're able to fight. Damn. Two of the Jenkins bunch might be dead or crippled. And Josh Bennett is dead. The Jenkins kid and I might be the only ones left to fight. The Jenkins kid ain't much of a fighter without his old dad and his brother. Lordy, lordy, that leaves only me."

He realized he was talking to himself and he shut up. But he couldn't stop thinking:

How could they get his property? He had a legal claim. Buy it? Well, maybe, if they offered him enough money. He wouldn't sell cheap, though. He'd worked too hard to make something of his place. No sir. As his uncles used to say, any piece of property could be bought for enough money, but some things come high. John Wesley's homestead would come high.

And what did that earl, or whatever the hell he was, want with the Turquoise Basin? Raise cattle? Probably. Being a rich earl he'd want to go into the cattle business in a big way. It took a hell of a lot of land to graze a couple thousand cows. He'd want to be a rich landowner who sat on the porch with a fancy drink in his hand and watched somebody else do the work. Like those rich Easterners who owned the Turkey Track outfit in New Mexico Territory.

Yeah, that was it. He wanted to own a big ranch in the United States. Out West. Maybe do a little hunting. Old Josh once said those Easterners would pay anything to get a shot at an elk or a bear. Boy, wouldn't they just love to get a shot at a cougar.

Old Earl, whatever the hell his name was, had big plans. And he was not an honest man. That was plain to see. He intended to own the whole basin, and he didn't intend to pay much for it. What would happen if he made John Wesley an offer and John Wesley turned him down? What would he do next? No telling. Valerie Mitchell said the Earl was planning to rob him. How?

And she wanted to rob the earl. Huh. The earl was robbing the government, the homesteaders, and everybody else he could. Wouldn't it be justice if somebody robbed him?

Naw. John Wesley really didn't know anything about the earl, only what Valerie Mitchell had told him. Besides, he didn't want to do anything illegal. He'd had his share of that. Naw. He'd go on about his work. See what happened.

The snow didn't stay on the ground long. A bright sun cleaned it off in two days. Now, John Wesley decided, was the time to finish riding the high hills, making sure all the cattle were down. His and Josh Bennett's. He was spending more time at the JB ranch now than at his own place, and he was riding JB horses more than he was riding his own. Most of the cattle were down on the plains now, but he had to keep riding to see that they came down in the right part of the country. The grass in the basin was good, and unless the winter was an unusually hard one, the cattle would winter well.

While he was riding, he was thinking about what Valerie Mitchell had said. He'd seen no sign of anyone representing an English Earl. He'd seen no new cabins started. Did she know what she was talking about? People had been known to talk and talk without understanding everything they said. Or maybe the Earl had changed his plans.

John Wesley couldn't help thinking about it. He'd sure like to know. He could go to town and see Valerie Mitchell, see if she had anything more to tell him. Yeah, he could spare half a day now. Just out of curiosity he'd do that.

On his way into Cloudcroft, he saw a wagon and two riders ahead of him. Lifting his horse to a lope he rode closer to see if they were anyone he'd recognize. Uh-oh. The Jenkins clan. All three of them. The old man was driving a team pulling a light spring wagon, and the two sons were horseback. John Wesley stayed well behind, but they saw him. Old Man Jenkins "Whoaed" the team, turned in his seat and looked back at him. The two boys turned their horses around facing him.

Here it comes, John Wesley thought, and a knot of fear formed in his stomach. Now was their chance to get even. The old man and his older son had either healed fast or they weren't hit bad. But they knew damn well who'd shot them and they couldn't let any man get by with that. He was in open country, not a tree or a gulley in sight.

There was no chance he could outshoot all three. Not in a stand up gunfight. What to do? Drop off his horse and hit the ground? Shoot from a prone position? He'd be a smaller target that way. What would they do, gun him down and claim it was self-defense? Naw. They had no fear of the law. They'd just shoot him down and say nothing to anyone.

John Wesley raised his right foot out of the stirrup, ready to get down and drop flat. Or—he suddenly remembered that he'd outshot them once from the back of a running horse. Maybe he could do it again.

With a rebel yell, he spurred his mount into a dead run, reining around the wagon, about a hundred and fifty yards south of it. He leaned low over the horse's neck with the Army Colt in his hand. The horse was running hard, doing what it was asked to do. Any second now, Old Man Jenkins was going to pick up a rifle and take aim. The two sons would open fire, too. John Wesley clung to his horse and watched, expecting it. If they shot his horse down he'd use the horse's body for a fortress. And if they shot his horse, he'd kill all three of them if he could. To his way of thinking shooting a horse was as bad as shooting a man.

He was ready.

Nothing happened.

They just watched him. Made no move to aim a gun. When he was two hundred yards ahead he reined the horse back to the wagon road and slowed to a trot.

Looking back he saw that the Jenkinses still hadn't moved.

Well now, that was strange. John Wesley kept his horse at a steady trot on into Cloudcroft. Every time he looked back the old man and his two sons were coming at a walk. Damned strange. By the time he got to the outskirts of town they were a mile or more behind him.

This didn't make sense. They had a reason to want to kill him. They'd killed Old Josh for no reason at all.

Puzzled, John Wesley rode down the main street, trying to figure it out. Traffic was light, but the horse, unaccustomed to the sights and smells of town, had its head up and its ears twitching, ready to bolt at the sight of anything scary. Knowing he could handle the horse, John Wesley rode relaxed, still trying to understand it all.

He rode past the courthouse, turned the horse around and went back. Dismounting, he tied the horse to a hitchrail, hoped it wouldn't rear back and break the reins, and went down the stone steps to the sheriff's office. Maybe Sheriff Watkins would have something to say about Josh Bennett's murder. The sheriff wasn't there. Instead, John Wesley was greeted by a note on the door. "Gone to Rosebud. Be back Saturday. Sheriff Joseph Watkins."

Well, hell. All right, he'd go to the hotel and see Valerie Mitchell. That's what he'd come to town for anyway.

The hotel clerk gave him another critical looking-over when he stepped inside, said he believed Miss Mitchell was in her room but John Wesley would have to wait in the lobby. He would go up and ask Miss Mitchell if she wanted to see him.

John Wesley waited. Stood on first one foot and then the other and waited. The sour-faced clerk came down frowning. Miss Mitchell would be down shortly, he said.

Waited some more.

When she came down, finally, she nodded at John Wesley and approached the clerk. "Mr. Budeen and I have some business to discuss," she said. "We need privacy. We are going up to my room."

"Miss Mitchell, we, the hotel, disapprove of guests entertaining visitors of the opposite sex."

"I'm not entertaining anyone, and you can go ahead and disapprove. Come on, Mr. Budeen."

The clerk's face turned red and he suddenly busied himself with papers on his desk. John Wesley followed her up the stairs. She was dressed like a lady, looked like a lady, but when she wanted to she could talk like a hardnosed businessman.

Nothing fancy about the hotel room. The bed was iron with springs and a mattress. It hadn't been made since it was slept in last. A woman's clothes hung in an open closet, and a woman's make-up was scattered over the top of a chiffonier. Valerie Mitchell wasn't a very good housekeeper. She made a half-hearted attempt at straightening the bed, then sat on it.

"Sit," she said.

He sat in the wooden chair, holding his hat in his lap. "You've been thinking about what I said, Johnnie. What is your answer?"

"My answer is the same, Miss Mitchell, but I, uh, I haven't seen hide nor hair of any English earl or anybody who represents him, and I wonder, uh, I wonder if there's anything new."

"There is. I've been in touch. Don't ask me how. But there is something new. That is, there will be."

Turning his hat around in his hands, John Wesley had to ask, "What?"

She shook her head. "I can't tell you everything unless I have your promise to help me rob the bastard."

"Well, then, I reckon I'll just have to wait and see."

"You won't have to wait long." She was leaning back, with her hands on the bed behind her, smiling that half-smile again.

His eyes went over the room, taking in everything, back to her. It was the first time in two years that he had been alone in a room with a woman. And this one was damned pretty. Not so much a lady either. He couldn't help thinking about it. She read his thoughts.

"The way you live, you get lonely, don't you, Johnnie?"

111

Without waiting for an answer, she went on, "Think of what you could do with a lot of money. No more working your butt off trying to hack out a living. You could be in Denver or Albuquerque, living high, taking your pick of pretty girls."

He didn't know what to say.

"You're a good-looking fella, Johnnie. If you were cleaned up and dressed up you'd be a real lady killer."

On a sudden impulse, so sudden he didn't even think of what he was doing, he got up, moved over and sat on the bed beside her. He started to put an arm around her when she jumped up.

Chuckling, she said, "Not here, Johnnie. If you want to make love to me you have to get a haircut and some nice clothes. And it has to be in a better place than this."

Embarrassed, he stood, stuttering, "I, uh, didn't expect, uh, well..."

With her head cocked to one side, she asked, "Why did you come here, Johnnie? Really? You can't contain your curiosity, can you?"

"Yeah, yes, I reckon that's it."

She walked to the one window, looked out, turned back, frowning, seeming to be deep in thought. Finally, "All right, I'll tell you something, something very important."

He waited for her to go on.

"I'll say just a few words now and no more. Don't even ask me to tell you more. Agreed?"

"All right."

"Someone...someone is going to be killed."

CHAPTER 16

When he came out of the hotel, the senior Jenkins was sitting in his wagon across the street in front of the mercantile. His sons came out of the store carrying bags of flour and sugar. They were stocking up for the winter. John Wesley could sure use some groceries. That was one of the things he wanted to see the sheriff about. Had he located Josh Bennett's heirs? If so, would the heirs honor Josh's debts? If Valerie Mitchell knew he'd helped Josh drive a herd of cattle to the railroad, others probably knew. He could prove Josh had owed him money. And boy did he need it.

In another week or so he'd have to sell some more calves.

He stood across the street from the Jenkinses watching them and wondering if the old man had a bullet wound that kept him from getting out of the wagon. The Jenkins boys saw him standing there and stopped what they were doing and watched him.

Matching them stare for stare was getting nowhere so John Wesley untied his horse, mounted, and rode out of town. All the way back to the JB ranch, the thoughts he couldn't get out of his mind were: did Valerie Mitchell know what she was talking about?

If so, who was going to be killed? And how?

All of John Wesley's W Bar cattle and Josh Bennett's JB connected cattle were grazing along a ten mile stretch of Turkey Creek now. Because they knew where the water was, they wouldn't stray more than a day's walk away. Unless they were driven south by a snow storm. Cattle liked to turn their tails to the wind and drift away from it. In the spring, cattlemen spent long days on horseback, rounding up their cattle and branding their calves.

In the plains country, cattlemen organized spring roundups and worked together, each outfit making certain that no one branded the wrong calves. In the Turquoise Basin there weren't enough cattlemen to organize. Besides, the Jenkins family and their Broken O outfit wouldn't work with anyone. They'd do things their way whether anyone liked it or not. Lord help the man who slapped his brand on a calf that was sucking a Broken O cow.

John Wesley went back to his own outfit, cut out two of his calves and put them in the corral. Tomorrow he'd drive them to town and sell them to whoever wanted to butcher them. He'd have to drive them to town by himself. Josh Bennett wasn't around anymore.

Thinking of Old Josh made him feel even lonelier as he cooked his supper, ate, and washed the dishes. And loneliness made him think again of Valerie Mitchell. She could talk like a saloon woman, but she knew how to be a lady, too. How would she like living on a cow ranch? Naw, she'd made it clear she liked the finer things in life, the things that cost money. Best forget her. That shifted his thoughts back to Josh Bennett. The anger returned. Old Josh lying dead in the grass, shot in the back. The goddam Jenkinses. Those murdering sons of bitches.

Next day he had cause to wonder whether the Jenkinses really did it. It wasn't only what happened, it was that and what Valerie Mitchell had said.

The calves were not giving him as much trouble as he'd expected, and he had hopes he could get them to town in good shape. When he got there he'd put them in a pen at the livery and let it be known at the mercantile and the saloon that he had young beeves for sale.

The sun was up high, and an Indian summer had followed the first snow. How long it would last was anybody's guess, but John Wesley enjoyed the warmth of the sun. At mid-afternoon, only a few miles from town, he looked back and saw riders coming. There were about a dozen riders and a wagon pulled by a two-horse team. As

114

slow as he was traveling, allowing the calves to take their time, it wasn't long before the riders and wagon caught up to him. The sheriff was among them, his silver badge glinting in the sunlight. The men's faces were grim, and when the wagon drew abreast he would see why. Three bodies lay in the back, covered with a greasy tarp.

John Wesley let the calves go and reined over beside the sheriff. "Who?" was all he said.

Sheriff Joseph Watkins glanced his way, then looked straight ahead. "Mr. Jenkins and his two sons."

"What?"

No one else spoke. John Wesley had to let that soak in before he could croak another question, "What happened?"

Still looking straight ahead, the sheriff said, "They resisted arrest. These men can attest to that."

"Resisted arrest? What were you gonna arrest them for? Josh's murder?"

Sheriff Watkins looked at him then with sad eyes. "No, all I wanted to do was to talk with them. That's all I wanted."

Another man spoke, a man with a stubby beard and a six-gun carried low. "They must've been guilty or they wouldn't have shot at us."

John Wesley asked, "Did you find some evidence that pointed to them?"

His horse and the sheriff's horse walked side by side. Sheriff Watkins turned his head and looked long and hard at John Wesley. "You believe they killed your neighbor, don't you?"

"Yeah, but—"

"Don't you think I should have talked with them about it?"

"Sure but—"

"Well, that's what I wanted to do. I went out there yesterday just to talk with them, and they shot at me. They didn't even wait to see what I was there for, just opened fire. I was lucky to get away alive."

John Wesley absorbed that, then, "All three of them? They all shot at you?"

"Yep. One was in the yard by the house when I started to ride up. He ran inside the house and all three of them poked gun barrels through the windows."

"Did they say anything?"

"Yeah, they told me to git. They didn't give me a chance to say anything myself." The sheriff seemed to be on the defensive, wanting to convince John Wesley that what had happened was unavoidable. It was something he'd have to repeat a dozen times in the future.

Riding quietly for a moment, John Wesley guessed the rest. The sheriff couldn't allow anyone to get by with shooting at an officer of the law and he gathered a small army and went back this morning. The Jenkinses had fought it out and lost the battle.

The man with the stubby beard spoke again, "We had to burn the house down. They wouldn't come out 'til the smoke drove 'em out, and they came out shootin'."

Looking at the faces around him, John Wesley recognized only two. They were two men he'd seen in the saloon. The others he'd never seen before. But then he didn't get to town very often and knew very few men around Cloudcroft. He rode side by side with the sheriff for another moment, then dropped back.

It was nearly dark when he got the calves penned at the livery, and everyone was too excited about the shooting to think about buying beeves. At the mercantile, he let the proprietor know he had calves for sale, then went to the saloon to tell the bartender.

"Hey, Budeen." It was a rancher from over west of town, a man John Wesley had met before in the saloon. "Hear about your neighbors?"

"Yeah, I heard."

"Expect you're glad to git rid of them Jenkinses."

Speaking sourly, John Wesley answered, "Yeah, I reckon."

"They was trouble. Heard they tried to shoot you out of your cabin once."

"Yeah."

"Heard the sheriff thinks they backshot Old Josh Bennett."

"Yeah."

"Have a drink of whiskey on me."

"Well, uh, thanks, but I brought a couple of calves to town to sell, and I've got to get back to the livery pens." He turned to the bartender, a man with thick hair parted in the middle and a handlebar moustache. "If you hear of anybody who wants to buy some calves, send them over to the livery pens."

"Sure, I'll do that."

Barney Howser, the livery owner, agreed to let John Wesley wait until after the calves were sold to pay for the hay they ate. "If I'm lucky they'll be sold by noon tomorrow," John Wesley said, "but in the meantime they have to eat. And I have to get back to my homestead. Tell everybody the price is thirteen bucks apiece, and collect the money for me, will you."

"I'll do 'er," the livery owner said. "Whatta you think about them Jenkinses? Heard they gave you fits once."

"Yeah. They weren't friends with anybody."

"Do you believe it? That they bushwhacked Josh Bennett?"

"I don't know who else could have done it, but..." John Wesley shook his head sadly. And as he mounted his horse and started home in the dark, he suddenly realized he was no longer convinced that the Jenkinses were guilty.

Why was he no longer convinced? He ran it through his mind over and over. One, Valerie Mitchell said someone was going to die. Valerie Mitchell had said a lot of things. Two, when he thought it over carefully, he had to admit he never had any proof that Old Man Jenkins and his two sons were bushwhackers. He had plenty of reason to suspect them, but that was all, just a suspicion. With reins hanging slack, the horse headed for home.

The closer to home they got the faster the horse walked. But who else would have done it and why? That woman, Valerie Mitchell, knew someone was going to die. How did she know? Or was it somebody else who was going to die?

Even after he was at home in his bunk with his hands under his head, staring at the dark ceiling, he worried about it. Somehow the death of the Jenkins clan was sad. It wasn't something to celebrate. No, when he turned it over in his mind, he was not happy about the end of the Jenkinses.

He tried to put himself in Old Man Jenkins's place. He'd come to this basin as a young man with a young wife. The Indians were still running wild and killing everyone they could catch. Young Jenkins fought them off. By hard work and keeping a gun handy, he'd built himself a cow outfit. Over the years two sons were born. Sometime after that, Mrs. Jenkins died. Mr. Jenkins taught his boys hard work, and he taught them how to protect themselves with a gun. There was no law. A man had to protect himself. A man had to take the law into his own hands. And when the territory was divided into counties, and sheriffs were elected, some of the lawmen were no more honest than the thieves and killers. A man had to make his own law.

Then the land was opened up to homesteading. Homesteaders, looking for free land, moved in. First it was Josh Bennett, and a few years later John Wesley Budeen. The Jenkinses had grazed their cattle all over the northern end of the Turquoise Basin, and now somebody else's cattle were grazing there. Grass that the Jenkins family had reserved for winter was now being cropped off by other men's cattle.

How would he, John Wesley Budeen, feel if he had been in Old Man Jenkins's place? It would be hard to be neighborly to folks who were taking over some of his country. Yeah, John Wesley admitted to himself, he would probably be unfriendly, too.

But there was the time the Jenkinses tried to shoot him out of his cabin. They'd claimed he'd butchered one of their steers, but they couldn't produce the carcass. That was being more than just unfriendly.

"Huh," John Wesley snorted out loud. That was being downright murderous. And the three men who'd tried to shoot him out of the saddle during a small cattle stampede. They weren't just protecting their grazing land then. And Josh Bennett's murder. Who else but the Jenkinses?

And now. Sheriff Joseph Watkins seemed to be a fair and honest man who really cared about justice. He'd always been sensible and logical. Now he was a party to the death of the Jenkins family. They didn't even allow him to say what he went there to say. Just started shooting. It would be easy to believe they had something to hide.

For the first time in years, John Wesley wished he had a chaw of tobacco. Or a drink of whiskey. Or at least more coffee. Something to do besides lie here and try to figure this out. He had to figure it out.

He wouldn't be any good for anything else until he had this whole damned thing straight in his mind.

CHAPTER 17

One calf had been sold by mid-morning. The other stood in the pen chewing hay. Barney Howser handed John Wesley thirteen dollars. It wasn't a lot of money, but it would buy a few groceries, some coffee and a slab of bacon, if nothing else.

"There was a gent here lookin' at this 'un, this heifer," the livery owner said. "Thought the price was too high. I told 'im you was just tryin' to make a livin' like ever'body else. Said he'd think on it."

"That's a lot more beef than he can buy in a store for thirteen dollars."

"Said he was thinking about lettin' her grow up enough to come fresh and makin' a milk cow out of 'er." At that John Wesley had to grin. "I reckon if she had a calf she'd give milk. And I reckon if somebody made a pet of her she'd stand to be milked."

"Lots of cows around here, but damned few milk cows."

"If that's what he wants to do, I'll sure sell her to him."

"He might be back."

Sheriff Joseph Watkins wasn't in his office, but when John Wesley went out to the street again he saw him coming. "Morning," the paunchy sheriff said. "Morning."

"Whatta you say this fine fall morning? Or is it early winter?"

"I don't know what the government experts call it," John Wesley drawled, trying to be conversational, "but that snow we had a few days ago looked like winter to me."

"It's that time of year. Got something on your mind?"

"Yeah, a couple of things."

"Come on in."

Inside, the sheriff plopped himself into a chair, tilted the chair back on its hind legs and parked his boots on the desk. John Wesley sat down in a straight-backed chair. "I was wondering if you found any of Josh Bennett's kin."

"Found a letter from a sister in Amarillo, Texas. I sent a wire to the sheriff down there and ask him to break the news to her. Ought to be hearing from her pretty soon."

"Hope so. He owed me some money for some work I did for him. I sure could use it."

"I heard you helped him trail some cattle to the railroad, and now you're wearin' out saddle leather for the benefit of his heirs. Soon's the district judge comes to town I'm gonna turn the property over to him to worry about. He'll probably arrange to pay you for takin' care of everything."

"I'd appreciate that. I'm selling a couple of calves, but that won't get me through the winter."

"We're burying Mr. Bennett this afternoon, you know. Can't keep a body very long. We've kept this one too long already. We won't open the casket."

"Can I help? I've got a few bucks, and I want him to have a good funeral."

"You can pay the preacher, a gentleman name of Benjamin from the Baptist Church. He'll preach for nothin' if he has to, but he'd rather be paid. Old Sam keeps some pinewood coffins ready for when they're needed. The Parson will preach longer and his wife and daughter will sing if they get paid for it. And Old Sam has better-lookin' coffins. If you want to pay we won't have to bury him in a pauper's grave."

"Yeah, I'll pay as much as I've got."

"Good. I'll tell 'em and let them settle with you." The sheriff's feet came down from the desk. But before he could stand, John Wesley asked:

"Uh, Mr. Watkins, I can't help thinking about the Jenkinses. Do you have any idea why they shot at you?"

"Why do you ask? I'd think you'd be glad to get rid of 'em."

"Oh, I don't know. They were never friendly, that's for sure, but...I just can't see them shooting at you without letting you explain why you went there."

Sheriff Watkins's face suddenly hardened and his eyes narrowed. "That's what they did. I've got witnesses. Of course I couldn't let 'em get by with shooting at a duly elected officer of the law. What kind of law would we have around here if we let folks get by with that? I got some men and went back. Hell, they started shootin' as soon as we came in sight."

All John Wesley could do was shake his head. Then another question popped into his mind. "Who were all the men? I recognized only two of them."

"Men I recruited off the street. I've got authority to do that. I told 'em what the deal was and asked for volunteers. Hell, there was plenty of volunteers. The Jenkinses had enemies."

"Yeah," John Wesley said thoughtfully, "I reckon they did."

"I've got to go back out there today and take inventory, then I've got to try to find some heirs again." The sheriff's face had softened somewhat. "I can guess what you're thinking, a pioneer family being wiped out like that. It's too bad. I didn't want to do it."

"Did somebody say their house burned down?"

"Yeah. It was the only way we could get 'em out. That house was like a fort. Only thing left is the chimney. There won't be any letters from kinfolk. I don't know how I'm going to find a kin."

"Somebody around here must know something about them."

"I'm asking. I hope you're right."

The funeral was a good one. Reverend Benjamin preached about life and death and said Mr. Josh Bennett had gone to a peaceful valley prepared by the Savior. The reverend and his family sang "Rock of Ages," and "There Is A Valley." The service ended after the reverend opened his Bible, read the twenty-third psalm, and prayed with tears running down his cheeks. Twenty-six townspeople listened with bowed heads and left as men began shoveling dirt into the grave. A hand-carved cross was driven into the ground at the head of the mound. The message on the horizontal piece said simply, "Joshua Bennett A Fine Gentleman RIP."

John Wesley paid the preacher and his family first, then the grave diggers and the coffin-maker. He was a dollar short, but he promised the coffin-maker he would pay the dollar as soon as he sold another calf.

Then he rode home, broke, with very few groceries left, and no coffee. "Aw well," he said to his horse, "I couldn't let him be buried a pauper. He was a friend."

It was three days later that he sold the heifer. A townsman with a family to feed paid twelve dollars for her. John Wesley allowed himself to be talked down in price when the man said he intended to raise the heifer until she was grown enough to breed, then get a calf from her and milk her. The heifer was lucky. She would live a good life. After paying the livery owner for the feed, and Sam for Josh's coffin, he went to the mercantile and bought some feed for himself. Boy, wouldn't some coffee taste good. He'd stock the cupboard at his cabin and at the JB Ranch, too. That way he'd have coffee and chuck wherever he spent the night. But he knew the money wouldn't last long. Unless Josh Bennett's heirs paid him he'd have to sell a couple more calves.

"Huh," he said to himself with a wry grin, "I'm eating up my profits."

Two days later Valerie Mitchell came calling again.

He was building a roof over his haystack when he saw her coming. She was riding astraddle in a man's saddle, wearing the split skirt and the black hat. He climbed down from his homemade ladder and went to meet her.

"Morning."

She said nothing until she'd dismounted. Then, "Are you ready? Time is running out."

Grinning, John Wesley drawled, "I've got plenty of time. That's about the only thing I've got." He was glad to see her, see anyone.

But she was serious. "It has to be done soon. It has to be timed right."

He knew what she was talking about, but he asked anyway, "What has to be done soon?"

"Don't exasperate me, Johnnie. That could be bad for your health."

His grin vanished. "Are you threatening me?"

"I'm not threatening you, I'm warning you."

"Well, just tell me how it would be bad for my health."

Her shoulders slumped. She looked weary. "Can we go inside? We have to talk."

Studying her, he could see her face was troubled. She looked to be under pressure of some kind. "All right. Here, let me tie up your horse."

Glad that he had swept the floor that morning, he pulled a chair away from the table and invited her to sit.

She leaned back in the chair with her feet in front of her. "Care for a cup of coffee?" he asked. "There's still some heat in the stove and it won't take long to warm up."

"That would be wonderful."

He lifted a lid off the stove, stirred the hot ashes and put the coffeepot over the open top. "I've even got some canned cream, if you like cream in your coffee."

"Cream would be fine."

He sat on his bunk again, waiting for her to say whatever she'd come to say.

"What I meant by a warning, Johnnie, was, well, men have been killed in this area recently."

"Uh-huh."

"Mr. Bennett was shot in the back."

"Yeah?" He believed she was about to say something damned interesting.

"It was planned."

"Planned?"

"Yes. Mr. Jenkins and his sons were not responsible."

"Oh yeah? Then who the hell was?"

"Is the coffee hot yet? I left town without breakfast."

"I think it is. But—"

"Please, Johnnie."

He stood, and, using a piece of a flour sack to protect his hand from the heat, lifted the coffeepot off the stove. He poured two tin cups full and added a few drops of condensed milk from a can. Handing her a cup, he said, "All right, talk."

She took a sip, put the cup on the table. "It was part of the

123

Earl's scheme. Gaining control of the Turquoise Basin is easy if he can get rid of you three."

"Us three?"

"Sure. You, Mr. Bennett, and the Jenkins family."

"Are you saying he shot Josh Bennett?"

Shaking her head, she said, "Of course not. He wouldn't dirty his own hands. He hired it done."

"He paid somebody to kill Josh Bennett?"

"Yes." She picked up the coffee cup and took another sip.

"Lordy, lordy." He put his cup on the floor, put his chin in his hands and tried to comprehend. It couldn't be. An English earl paid somebody to kill Josh Bennett. Why Josh Bennett? The Jenkinses had the biggest outfit. They'd be the meanest to deal with. Why Old Josh? The answer came to him.

"Oh-h-h," he groaned.

"You're beginning to see it, aren't you, Johnnie?"

"God, oh God."

"I told you he's a schemer. There's nothing he won't do."

"That leaves only me."

Nodding, she said, "It does, doesn't it?"

He stood, stomped across the room and back and stopped in front of her. "What does he figure on doing about me?"

She looked up at him. "I honestly don't know, Johnnie. All I knew is that he planned for someone to be killed and his goal was to own all of Turquoise Basin."

"But you're sure about who killed Josh Bennett?"

"I know it was someone he hired."

"Who told you?"

"I can't tell you, Johnnie. If the earl found out he'd seen me his life would be in danger."

"Somebody close to this earl, or whatever he is?"

"That is correct."

Stomping across the room and back again, he muttered, "Boy, oh boy."

"There is one defense, Johnnie."

Again, he stopped in front of her. "Yeah?"

"You know what it is."

"Sure, I could shoot holes in him. That is if I could find him. Or I could...like you said, I could rob him before he robs me."

"Exactly."

"Where can I find him?"

"Are you with us?"

"Who is us?"

"My friend who is close to the earl."

"Oh. You and your friend have cooked up a plan to rob this earl and you want me to help."

"Right again."

"Why do you need me?"

"If my friend did it he'd be a suspect immediately. It has to be done by an outsider."

"So he asked you to find somebody who wouldn't mind a little larceny."

"Not exactly. It was my idea."

Walking across the room again, slowly this time, John Wesley ran it through his mind. He sat on his bunk and stared at his coffee cup cooling on the floor. "Then you are close to this rich gent yourself."

"Was."

"You worked for him?"

"Let's just say, Johnnie, that the earl and I were as close as a man and woman can get."

"What happened?"

"He uses people."

"Uh-huh." It was easy to guess the rest.

Conversation halted for a moment while John Wesley conjured up a mental picture of Valerie Mitchell in bed with a rich English earl. It was easy to do, and for a second he was envious.

"All right," he said, finally, "what's to keep me from robbing your ex all by myself?"

She held up two fingers. "One, you don't know where he is, and two, you will have to have some help."

Another pause. "What do you say, Johnnie?"

"Huh-uh. I'm not in the robbing business."

Slowly, wearily, she stood. "I've wasted my time, haven't I?

I've spent a lot of time in the dreadful little burg of Cloudcroft for nothing."

"Why, Miss Mitchell? The earl doesn't live around here. If he did I'd have heard about him. Why are you staying in Cloudcroft?"

"It's...it fits our plan." Then she straightened her shoulders. "I'm not giving up. We do need your help, and I'm not giving up on you. You'll help us."

"What makes you think so?"

"You said it yourself, Johnnie. You're the only one left to fight them. They are going to make you so angry you'll do anything to hit back."

"You're sure this gent has hirelings who are going to do something, but you don't know what."

"If I did I'd tell you. The thing that worries me most, Johnnie, is they'll stop at nothing. They've demonstrated that. I worry that...I worry that you might not survive."

CHAPTER 18

He built the roof over his haystack with poles covered with pine branches. The branches were intertwined as tightly as he could get them. The roof, on four high tree trunk legs, slanted enough that most of the rain and snowmelt would run off instead of soak through. It was better than nothing.

When he worked Valerie Mitchell was on his mind. If they were partners in a crime maybe they would continue being partners. While he thought about her, he kept his eyes busy, looking up north at the mountains and down south toward Turkey Creek.

At night he began pushing the table and chairs against the cabin door and sleeping on the floor instead of on his bunk. If anyone poked a gun through the window and emptied it at the bunk, he wouldn't be in it.

He went to town, paid ten cents for a glass of beer, and asked the bartender if he'd ever heard of an English earl in these parts. The bartender looked at him as if he thought he was crazy. What would an English earl be doing around here? The sheriff wasn't in his office, and John Wesley considered going to the sheriff's house. Naw. He probably wasn't there either. Back to work.

He was at the JB Ranch, prying worn iron shoes off a horse when a one-horse buggy pulled into the yard. The man who got out was well-dressed in a Prince Albert coat, a cravat at his throat, and laced shoes. He was not armed. If this was the English earl, he sure didn't look dangerous. But he wasn't the earl. He introduced himself as Mr. Howard Weston, president of the Turquoise Valley Bank.

John Wesley shook hands with him. The man's hand was soft.

"I have been appointed by District Judge Dudley Iverson to administer the estate of the late Josh Bennett," he said. "I've been told by Sheriff Watkins that you have been looking after the assets of the estate."

"I've been gathering Josh's cattle, yeah. Have you found an heir?"

"Yes, as a matter of fact, we have. Mr. Bennett's sister in Amarillo, Texas. She has informed me that Mr. Bennett has a daughter."

"Yeah, he had a little girl."

"I wasn't informed of the child's age, only that Mr. Bennett's sister is the guardian of the next of kin. That does confuse things. The court will have to decide whether the sister is actually a legal guardian before we can do anything else."

That bit of information was a sour disappointment to John Wesley. "Well, I can do the work until somebody else comes along, but I could use some money. Josh was my friend and I'll do everything I can to keep his outfit in shape, but I don't owe his heirs anything."

"I understand, Mr. Budeen. I understand perfectly. I wish I could offer you some funds now, but I cannot. Only the rightful heir or her guardian can authorize payment to you."

"Yeah," he said peevishly, "and that means court hearings and everything else."

"I am afraid that's where things stand. I can guarantee you that you will be paid as soon as the estate is settled, but unfortunately I don't know when that will be."

"Sure, sure."

"Meanwhile, I, as duly appointed administrator of the estate, authorize you to continue working to protect the assets of the estate with the understanding that you will be adequately compensated when the affairs are settled."

"Sure, sure."

"Is that agreeable?"

"Does anybody object to me staying here at the ranch house?

It's easier to keep an eye on JB cattle from here."

"I have no objection at all."

"All right. But I hope you get this settled pretty quick. I feel like I'm trespassing."

It took two days to separate his cattle and Josh Bennett's from Broken O cattle that had drifted west. He pushed the Broken O stuff toward the Jenkinses' ranch. He saw no one representing the Broken O, and wondered when and if someone would come along and claim the property. Sheriff Joseph Watkins was waiting for him when he got back to the JB ranch.

"I see you're working hard," the paunchy sheriff said genially.

"It's mostly horseback work, the kind I like. What's new, Sheriff?" John Wesley dismounted and pulled the saddle off a thick-necked brown horse, a JB horse.

"Oh, just stopped on my way back to town. Went over to the Jenkins place to see that their horses were turned out and no animals were starvin'. Had to go to an inquest over in Rosebud a few days ago about the Jenkins bunch. Too bad about them."

"I reckon the district attorney or whoever runs things over there didn't give you any trouble."

"No. None at all. I took some witnesses with me. That's out of my jurisdiction over there, but we're in the same court district. The DA doesn't like to travel, so we had to go over there."

A question popped out of John Wesley's mouth before he had time to think: "How about the U.S. Government land agent? I hear he doesn't like to travel."

"Why do you ask that?"

"Oh, I just wondered. I had to go over to Rosebud myself when I filed my claim." Then another question came to his mind: "Say, Sheriff, I've been wanting to ask you, have you ever heard of an English earl around here?"

Two changes came over the sheriff's normally pleasant face. First, one of puzzlement, and then one of caution. "What? An English earl?"

"I believe his name is the Earl of Ravenshire."

"What about him?"

John Wesley shrugged. "Aw, there's a rumor that somebody

called the Earl of Ravenshire is doing a little land grabbing."

"Where'd you hear that?" The Sheriffs voice was suddenly sharp, snappy. His hands were on his hips.

"Just picked up some gossip."

"From who?" Still sharp.

Now John Wesley was puzzled. Why did Sheriff Joseph Watkins suddenly turn into a hard case? "Oh, I don't know, just talk, that's all."

"Talk from who?"

He'd thrown his saddle onto the top rail of a corral, and now he turned to face the sheriff. He didn't like the sheriff's tone and he decided he wasn't going to answer the question. "Just talk. All right?"

Again, a change came over Sheriff Joseph Watkins, only now he was forcing himself to smile. He slowly relaxed and let his hands hang down at his sides. John Wesley could see that it was an act.

"Well, the way you asked, I thought he might be somebody important. It's my job to hear about anybody important moving in."

"Sure."

"Well, got to get back home. The woman who keeps house for me is lookin' for me about now. The sheriff mounted a roan mare, waved, and rode away, back stiff.

"Sure," John Wesley mused aloud when the sheriff was out of hearing range, "you've heard of him, all right." He remembered something his Uncle Ezekiel had once said: Watch a man's face. You can sometimes learn more from a man's face than from what he says. "Yeah," John Wesley repeated, "you've heard something. And you don't like me knowing about it. There has to be a reason."

He carried an armload of hay to the night horse and went into the house. After taking another look at the picture on Josh Bennett's dresser, he started cooking his supper. Sure, he thought, silently, there is a reason. If what Valerie Mitchell said is true, the earl, or whatever the hell he is, doesn't want anybody to know about his scheme. Not yet. Does the sheriff know? Sure, he does. Is he on the earl's payroll? Naw. Sheriff Joseph Watkins has always been an honest, fair-minded lawman. Everybody respects Sheriff Watkins. He's on the county payroll and nobody else's.

John Wesley wanted to believe that. He tried. But there were a couple of thoughts he couldn't push out of his mind: first, according to Valerie Mitchell, Josh Bennett was killed by somebody hired by Earl Whatsisname. That got rid of Josh Bennett. Second, it also got rid of the Jenkinses. In a roundabout way, Josh Bennett's murder resulted in the deaths of the Jenkins bunch.

It could have been part of the scheme.

Then another possibility jumped up: The Broken O steer that was supposed to have been stolen. Could it really have happened? Someone else could have butchered the steer and put the carcass under John Wesley's haystack. That damn near got John Wesley killed. Was that part of the scheme, too?

Naw. The Jenkinses were trigger-happy yahoos who wanted to get rid of him worse than any English earl did. There wasn't any carcass. The whole thing was just an excuse the Jenkinses used to shoot him out. And the three gunnies who tried to shoot him out of the saddle near the railroad, there were three of them and there were three Jenkinses. Those three had to have been Old Man Jenkins and his two sons.

Well, they could have been someone else—three ranihans who thought they saw a chance to steal some beef on the hoof.

Aw, who the hell knows. There were too many possibilities and not enough facts.

Thoughts were buzzing around in John Wesley's head like flies in a bottle. Frowning, he tried to stop the buzzing and look at what he knew to be the truth.

For instance, the Jenkinses were trigger happy. They believed in making their own law. They were not reasonable men. That was a fact.

But the sheriff knew that if a bunch of quickly deputized hard cases ordered the Jenkinses out of their house, there would damned sure be some lead flying. Sheriff Joseph Watkins knew they'd fight. That was a fact, too.

Did it prove anything?

Aw hell. A man can imagine all kinds of things.

But doubt was growing in John Wesley's mind about the Jenkinses' guilt.

* * *

The sky was overcast, threatening snow, when John Wesley ran in Josh Bennett's remuda, caught a fresh horse, and headed back to his own homestead. There, he chopped a double armload of firewood, got on the horse again and rode south, wanting to see how far the cattle had drifted. One small bunch was a good seven miles by his estimation from Turkey Creek. He hazed them back toward water, then went home. Snow began falling by the time he got home, but it didn't look like it would be a heavy snow. Hard to tell, though. Well, he was as ready for winter as he could be. Now that he was in his cabin early in the day it was a good time to roast the remainder of the venison ribs. They had to be roasted slowly.

While the ribs cooked he mixed a batch of biscuit dough, and when everything was nearly ready to eat he made gravy from the roast drippings, flour, and water. He had a good supper, topped off with two cups of coffee.

He'd kept busy all day and that was what he needed to do to keep from worrying. But now, with the dishes washed and nothing to do but sit or sleep, the worry was back. If Valerie Mitchell knew what she was talking about, something was going to happen. Josh Bennett and the three Jenkinses were all dead.

Was he going to be next? If they planned to kill him, how would they do it? Shoot him in the back and put the blame on somebody else? Hell, there was nobody else. If he were in their place, what would he do? The smart thing would be to make his death look like an accident. How could they do that?

Suddenly, John Wesley reached a decision. Moving fast, he gathered his two guns, some blankets and a bed tarp and blew out the lamp. Like a thief in the night, he carried everything to the timbered hill behind his cabin, past the spring and uphill a short distance. The dark sky was still spitting snow, but he could see the clouds moving. That was a good sign. The sky would probably be clear by morning.

Back in the timber, he wrapped himself in the blankets and tarp, his two guns wrapped up with him, and prepared to spend the night there. Grumbling to himself he said quietly:

"Goddam. Another goddam night under a goddam tree."

It saved his life.

CHAPTER 19

At first he wasn't sure. Clouds hid the moon and it was too dark to see anything. He'd been dreaming. He'd dozed off with danger on his mind, and now he was dreaming about it. He should go back to sleep. Nothing was going on down there.

He closed his eyes, squirmed inside the blankets until he found a more comfortable position and started to doze off again. Suddenly, he was wide awake. It wasn't a dream. He'd seen something move near his cabin.

Now he was sitting up, straining his eyes, trying to penetrate the dark. Yeah, there it was. Something moved. Blinking, he tried to make it out. A horse? Clouds moved and for a few seconds a half-moon turned a dim light on the world below. It wasn't a horse, it was a man. Two men. Maybe more.

Slowly, he unwrapped himself and his guns from the blankets. The moon disappeared. He sat on the blankets and watched tensely, eyes straining. There was movement, but he couldn't make out what it was.

Wheels creaked, wagon wheels. Somebody down there struck a match. For a few seconds it illuminated a man's face and the door to his cabin. What the holy hell were they doing?

Uh-oh. Another match was struck and a torch made with a cloth-wrapped, kerosene-soaked stick was lit and tossed inside the window. A glow came from inside the window, enough light that John Wesley could see his wagon shoved up against the cabin door.

The light danced. The interior of the cabin was burning. Now the walls and the roof were on fire, too, creating enough smoke to choke an elephant. The tarpaper on the roof burned like kerosene. So did the walls.

Men were standing back watching, men with rifles in their hands. He counted five. There were probably more in the dark. At least two were in back of the cabin.

Sitting still, he shivered. In spite of heat waves coming from the fire, his blood turned cold when he thought about it. If he'd been asleep in the cabin, he'd be nothing more than a cinder by now. They had him trapped inside, or at least thought they did. With the back end of the wagon against the door and men with guns outside the window and in back, he should have been trapped inside and burned to death.

It was an accident. Townspeople, when they heard about it, would shake their head sadly and say it was too bad. It wasn't the first time a cabin had burned down. All it took was a too-hot stove pipe to set a tarpaper roof on fire, or a kerosene lamp knocked over or a pipe left burning on a bed. Too bad about that young man. They wouldn't even be able to give him a decent burial. The inside of the cabin had been so hot that the body had burned completely. Plumb burned up. Nothing left at all. While John Wesley watched, the roof fell in. Flames shot seventy-five feet into the air, and burning embers scattered another fifty feet around the cabin. Men turned and ran to safety. Then two walls caved in. Ten minutes later the other walls fell. Now it was a certainty no body would be found.

Men stood back and watched, firelight dancing on their faces. He counted six now, none he recognized. There were men in big floppy hats, there were men in bill caps. Some wore pants and some wore bib overalls. Flames still shot up higher than their heads.

His cabin, his home, was gone. The hard work he had done, the timbers he had cut with an axe and dragged down from the hills, notched and carefully lifted into place. The roof he'd built. All gone.

Sitting with his feet in front of him, he watched. Flames were dying. The whole floor was nothing but red-hot coals. There were a few lumps of burning wood and the iron stove. Nothing was standing. Even the stove was red-hot, and misshapen. Yeah, the fire was so hot it partially melted the stove.

As the fire died down, men became shadows again. They moved back into the dark and disappeared. The moon was above a cloud again. The only thing visible was the glowing pile of rubble that had been his cabin. It would be a long time before it cooled down enough that men could poke around and look for a body. They wouldn't be surprised when they didn't find one.

For that matter, it would be a long time before the tragedy was discovered. Now that Josh Bennett was dead, nobody came out here to visit. Except Valerie Mitchell. Would she come back?

It seemed to John Wesley that he had spent half his life sitting under a tree waiting for daylight. It came slowly, showing itself first on the eastern rim of the world. Yeah, he said to himself, daylight was coming. The sky was turning lighter. Then he could see the tree tops. Sorely, stiffly, he stood and stretched. He imagined he could hear his limbs creak like a rusty gate hinge. That was the way he felt, like a rusty hinge, barely able to move.

The men were gone. His night horse was still in the corral. If he'd been killed the horse would have had to stand in the corral and starve. At first it was painful to walk, but he put one foot in front of the other and slowly made his way down the hill. Red embers popped. The stove sat lopsided, caved in. Nothing else was recognizable. His nose burned from the stench and his eyes watered.

No use looking for anything. Just get on the night horse and go. At least, he thought grimly, it had stopped snowing. The sun would shine.

Leaving the blankets and bed tarp rolled up under a tree, he carried his two guns as he rode toward the JB Ranch. Instead of following the dim wagon ruts, he stayed to the north, paralleling the ruts. If anyone was down there he wanted to see them before they spotted him. He saw no one.

Before going inside Josh Bennett's house, he took a careful look around. Tracks showed that men had been there and gone. No strange horses were in sight. He held the Army Colt in his hand with the hammer back when he opened the door and stepped inside. A burned match lay on the table where someone had lit the lamp. Nothing was out of place. Outside again, he threw some hay to his horse, went back inside and cooked a small pot of rolled oats for his breakfast. He had oatmeal with canned milk, bacon and coffee.

Had the men been there before or after the fire? Probably before. They wanted to be sure he wasn't there and was in his cabin. They wouldn't be back soon.

His meal over, he washed the dishes and went outside and sat on the ground beside one of the corrals. It was decision time again. While he sat there two of Josh's horses came up to get a drink out of a wooden trough Josh had built and filled with a pipe from a spring. The horses had to bite through a thin sheet of ice to get at the water. Grinning at the way Old Josh had made pets of his horses, John Wesley picked up a halter, walked up to one of the horses and slipped it over his head. He led the horse inside a corral and turned the night horse out. Then he went back and sat on the ground again, huddled inside his plaid mackinaw.

All right, John Wesley Budeen, he said to himself, you're in a fine mess. A fine pickle, his old mother would have said. They, whoever the hell they were, intended to kill him. They thought they had killed him. When they found out he was still alive they'd try again. No use going to the sheriff. The sheriff was the one who'd sicced them onto him. The sheriff, who didn't want anybody in the Turquoise Basin to know about the Earl of something-or-other, had schemed to remove him from the face of the earth. There was no one to turn to for help. He could leave the country or get killed. That was that.

Unless...

What was it his old Uncle Luke had once said? "You can't win a war by defending yourself," that's what he'd said. "You gotta take the war to the enemy."

John Wesley stood, brushed off the seat of his pants, caught and saddled the horse he'd just corralled. Valerie Mitchell wouldn't have to come to him. He'd go to her.

At first he thought he'd wait until dark and try to get into town and out without being seen. But on second thought he couldn't stay out of sight forever. Besides, it might be interesting to see who was surprised when he showed up in town. Again he paralleled the wagon road to the outskirts of Cloudcroft, then rode boldly down the main street, looking back at everyone who looked at him. One man, a man with a six-gun carried low, was saddling a horse near the livery barn when he looked up and saw John Wesley coming. He stared, blinked, and punched the shoulder of another man who was standing with his back to the street. Both men stared at him.

Riding right up to them, John Wesley looked down from his horse and said, "Morning, gents."

They said nothing, only stared with mouths open.

John Wesley dismounted. If this turned into a shooting match he didn't want to be on a horse that might stampede at the sound of a gunshot. "Have I met you gents before?"

"Why, uh, no, don't b'lieve so." Both men stood facing him, hands close to their gun butts.

"Well, the way you looked at me I wondered if you recognized me."

"No. No sir, can't say we have."

"How about you?" John Wesley said to the other man. "No. Don't rec'lect ever seein' you before."

He didn't believe them but unless he wanted to start shooting there was nothing he could do about it. If he was the first to draw and shoot, chances were he could shoot both of them before they could get their guns cocked. But that would give Sheriff Watkins a legitimate excuse to get rid of him. Besides, that wasn't what he'd come to town for. "Do you gents happen to know if the sheriff is in his office?"

"Why no, ain't seen 'im."

The livery owner came out of the barn then, saw the three men facing each other with hands close to their guns and stopped suddenly. He waited, face frozen, then relaxed with relief when he saw John Wesley turn away. John Wesley led the horse, keeping it between him and the men. A block farther down the street he mounted the horse and rode to the courthouse. The sheriff's office door was open.

Another stare. Sheriff Watkins couldn't keep the surprise out of his eyes. He opened his mouth, then shut it. John Wesley said nothing, just waited for the sheriff to say something.

"Why, uh." The sheriff seemed to have something stuck in his throat. "Good morning, Budeen." He was getting control of himself now. "What brings you to town?"

John Wesley drawled, "Just wanted to find out if you've heard any more from Josh Bennett's heirs."

"Yeah, yes. Howard Weston over at the bank said his sister is coming. Doesn't know when. How, uh, how are things out at your place?"

"Oh." John Wesley shrugged. "As well as can be expected." He turned on his heels and left.

The hotel clerk still had a sneer on his face. He'd go up and ask if Miss Mitchell wanted to see him, he said. He came right back with Valerie Mitchell behind him. She was dressed in a long dark skirt, a heavy wool sweater and a perky little lacy hat.

"We have business to discuss," she said to the clerk. "Come on up to my room, Mr. Budeen." She started up the stairs, stopped. "Oh, and please cancel my ticket on the stage line. I might be staying another day."

In her room, he saw two satchels closed and standing by the bed. The wardrobe was empty and the top of the chiffonier was bare. "Going somewhere?" he asked, closing the door behind him.

"Uh-huh, but not the way I was planning. You're ready now, aren't you?"

"I'm ready."

"What happened?"

"You don't know?"

"No. I suspected something would happen to you but I didn't know what."

"They burned down my cabin."

"Oh. I'm not surprised. If I'd known I would have warned you somehow." Her forehead wrinkled. "How did you escape?"

"I've got a strong sense of self-preservation."

"You surely do. How soon can we get started?"

"Depends on where we're going."

"To Rosebud. Over the mountains."

"Is that where this Earl Whateverhisnameis lives?"

"He stays there part of the time. He has a house there."

"And money?"

"Some of the time."

"How about now?"

"Yes. I've been informed that he is keeping a large amount of cash at his house now."

"Your friend told you?"

"Yes."

"All right. If we're going to get over the mountains between daylight and dark we'll have to start just before daylight."

"Where shall we start from?"

It took a moment for John Wesley to decide, then, "From the east edge of town. Can you meet me there at first light? Have you got a horse or will you have to get one from Barney Howser?"

"I'm afraid I was depending on you to furnish the horses. I can walk to the edge of town."

"Have you got some clothes? I mean the kind of clothes that, well you know, some warm clothes? It might be cold."

"I can buy some at the mercantile."

"No. No use getting people's curiosity up. I'll bring some men's clothes."

"Where can I change?"

"There won't be anybody around at the edge of town and you can change clothes right there. I won't look and the horses won't be interested."

"All right."

He turned and stopped before opening the door. "Are you sure? Are you sure you want to do this, go over the mountains on a horse? Are you sure there'll be money in this gent's house?"

Her chin came up. Her eyes held his. "Yes, Johnnie, to all three questions."

As he walked down the stairs and out to his horse he wondered if he could depend on her and if she knew what she was talking about. This could all be for nothing.

But, well hell, what did he have to lose.

CHAPTER 20

He rode down the wagon road, the stage road, taking a long look behind him every few minutes. Where the road forked off to the JB Ranch he stopped, turned his horse around and took another long look. If any of Sheriff Watkins's so-called deputies were following him they were invisible. They didn't want to gun him down on a main road anyway. Instead, they'd shoot him in the back in the hills the way they'd shot Josh Bennett. He was safe for the moment.

Stopping at the JB Ranch, he put Josh's saddle on a horse, went into the house, and gathered some of Josh's clothes and a mackinaw. He also gathered a double handful of the groceries he'd stashed there, leaving only enough for a few days. Then he put all that into a burlap grain sack, tied it to Josh's saddle, mounted and led the horse back to what was left of his cabin. The ashes were still hot and the stench still burned his nose. He found a stick in the woods behind the cabin and poked around in the ashes a while, but found nothing worth keeping. Even his tin plates and cups were melted and shapeless.

With a feeling of sorrow, he realized he had never had any family photos or letters or anything worth keeping. Men who knew how to take pictures and had the cameras, flash powder, and film were scarce. Josh Bennett's family picture had to have been taken in Rosebud or Denver, or maybe Amarillo.

He ran in his horses, caught his two best and the mule, then turned the others out. Take care of yourselves, fellers, he said under his breath. He pitched some hay to the two horses and the mule, then went to the blankets and tarp he'd stashed under a tree in back of his cabin. There he opened a tin of beef, ate, and sat. Just before dark, he ate a can of peaches and a thick slice of bread, and went to see that the two horses and the mule were fed. After that there was nothing to do but wait.

Lying in his blankets with half the tarp under him and the other half folded back over him, he stared at the tree tops and the sky and tried to convince himself that robbing the Earl of England, or wherever he was from, was the smart thing to do.

He'd robbed before and gotten away with it, but he'd been damned lucky then. He remembered it clearly.

Smith—he never for a second believed that that was the man's real name—held a double-barreled shotgun on the tellers while he went behind the tellers' cages and filled two saddlebags with greenbacks. The tellers were so scared they never opened their mouths and didn't move. John Wesley left first and got mounted, holding the saddlebags across the fork of his saddle. He held Smith's horse ready. Smith backed out through the bank door and vaulted into the saddle, and they were on their way out of town, riding at a dead run. There were no shouts behind them. People on the street stared at them, but made no threatening moves.

They followed the road a few miles then cut north across country. They rode to the bottom of a shallow draw and stopped. Smith got down and, bending low, walked back to the south edge of the draw and studied their backtrail. He returned with a broad smile on his face.

"Ain't nobody comin'. What'd I tell you? We got away slicker'n a whistle."

"They'll be coming," John Wesley said. "But we'd best take it slow 'til we see 'em. Try to keep our horses strong."

"How much we got there?"

John Wesley dismounted and crawled to the edge of the draw. "Go ahead and count it. I'll watch."

He watched, eyes narrowed, expecting to see a bunch of riders coming from town, coming fast.

"Praise the Lord and hallelujah. We got better'n two thousand dollars here. Boy oh boy am I gonna live high."

"Let's go," John Wesley said, walking back and picking up his reins. "Not at a run, but traveling."

They angled north toward the Black Mountains and stopped in the late afternoon at a spot they'd picked out two days before. There they changed clothes and divided the money. John Wesley pulled the saddle off his horse so it could rest better. He led the horse to a stream that poured out of the mountains, let it drink, then tied it on a thirty foot rope where it could graze. He spent the rest of the day sitting under a man-high boulder watching back the way they'd come.

At dark he saddled his horse. "Let's ride."

"Why? Ain't nobody comin'."

"They're coming. I don't know why we haven't seen them, but they're coming. They know this country better than we do."

"Naw. Shit, let's have some grub."

"I'm riding."

"Well, shit, go on ahead. Shit, with different clothes and everything I might ride back to town tomorrow and take a stage to Lordsburg. Shit, I can pay."

John Wesley pulled the cinch snug but not too tight.

He wanted all the energy he could get from the horse. "That would be a damn fool thing to do. Me, I'm quitting the country as fast as this horse can carry me."

"Well, shit go on ahead. I'm catchin' a few winks and goin' back to town."

"Good luck to you, Smith."

"You too, Budeen."

John Wesley headed uphill, hoping the horse could see better than he could. He stayed on the trail for only a quarter-mile then turned west and north, following the creek.

A half-hour after he left he heard the gunshots.

For the rest of the night, he rode wherever the horse could go, wherever the hills were not too steep, nor the brush too thick, keeping generally north.

They had found Smith easily. It was easy because they knew that range of mountains, knew all the trails and likely camping spots.

It was easy to ask someone coming down the road if the two outlaws had been that way, and it was easy to figure that they had headed for the high country. The sheriff and his deputies had ridden into the mountains close to town and had come up behind Smith. Now they were looking for John Wesley Budeen.

Maybe not.

He'd worn a big floppy hat that nearly covered his face, and he'd stuck some horsehair to his cheeks with a paste made of flour and water. He didn't think he was recognizable. But they were looking for a second man, and if they saw John Wesley they'd be suspicious. Suspicious, hell. Some of the paste was still stuck to his face, and he had some of the bank's money in his saddle bags. He couldn't let anyone see him.

At daylight he unsaddled the horse and staked him out near a creek where the grass was high. The horse grazed for a few hours, then dozed, standing hipshot, legs locked the way only a horse can lock them. But John Wesley got no sleep. He sat near a pile of boulders on a high hill where he could see his backtrail, and was afraid to sleep.

Damn, he said to himself, this ain't worth it. No amount of money is worth this.

He continued north, staying away from town. After five days he came across two silver prospectors in their camp. He bought some grub from them. They asked him where he came from, and he lied and said he had come from the east and thought he was taking a shortcut to the town of Julesville. They didn't ask any more questions. While he was in their camp he borrowed a razor and shaved, then he washed his clothes in a galvanized washtub, walking around in his underwear while the clothes dried. When he left their camp he no longer looked like a man who had been traveling hard. He attracted no attention when he rode into Julesville.

Next morning, while he was eating breakfast in a hotel restaurant, he read in the Julesville newspaper about a bank robbery at Silverton and the killing of one of the robbers. The other robber got away, and his identity was unknown.

Still, it worried him. Could it be the newspaper reporter wasn't told everything? Lawmen were tricky. He wouldn't put it past them to pretend they didn't know who they were looking for. That would make the wanted man feel safe, and he might get careless. It ate on John Wesley. He didn't want to be a fugitive. If he could he'd give the money back and forget the whole thing. In Julesville, he walked the streets for three days and every time he saw a man with a badge pinned to his shirt, he felt like running. No one gave him a second glance.

Finally he couldn't stand it anymore. He had to go back and find out.

He was glad he did.

Now he was about to commit another robbery.

It wasn't the first time John Wesley had caught and saddled horses in the dark. The Turkey Track outfit often had to roll out of their beds early, saddle up in the dark and sit around and wait for daylight. That's the way cowbosses liked to do things. He put his saddle on one horse, Josh Bennett's on another horse and the crossbuck saddle and panniers on the mule. Josh's clothes, the grub, picket ropes, and hobbles went into one pannier and his bed tarp and blankets went into the other. It was a light load for the mule, but it, with riders, would have been too heavy and awkward for the horses.

The sky was clear and the air was cold. He huddled inside his mackinaw as he rode west, leading the extra horse and the mule. He reckoned it was about an hour and a half to daylight. While he rode he wondered whether Valerie Mitchell would be there. If she was he'd go along with her plan. If she wasn't...   He had no idea what he'd do if she failed him. He couldn't stay in the Turquoise Basin and defend himself forever.

The eastern horizon was just beginning to turn light when he reached the outskirts of Cloudcroft. At first he didn't see her. She was standing under a ponderosa pine, hugging herself and stamping her feet to keep warm.

"Thank God," she said through chattering teeth when he rode up. "I'm worn out from carrying this satchel and I'm completely frozen."

Dismounting, he dug Josh Bennett's clothes and mackinaw

from one of the panniers and handed them to her. "Here. This will help."

"Be a gentleman, will you please, and look the other way."

Standing with his back to her, a horse between them, he waited patiently while she changed. He wanted to look, take a quick peek, but, naw. The light on the eastern horizon was getting brighter. It was time to get started. Finally, she said, "All right. I'm decent again." She looked like a little man in Josh's clothes, which were three or four sizes too big for her. The floppy hat she wore with her blond hair tucked under it. Josh's red checkered mackinaw covered her from chin to knees.

The satchel she'd carried went into a pannier, the lightest one, and he tied the two panniers down with a lash cinch. While he was doing that, she mounted the extra horse. Josh's stirrups were too long for her, but the leathers were laced up and it would take time to unlace them, adjust them to the right length and lace them again. He should have done that the day before when he had time on his hands, but he hadn't thought about it.

"What did you tell the hotel clerk?"

"I told him I was going to visit some friends and was leaving in a buggy early this morning. I left one of my traveling cases in the room and paid for three more days and nights. He won't be surprised when he finds me gone."

Turning his horse around, he rode east, leading the mule. She followed. "You sure went to a lot of trouble for this job, Miss Mitchell. It must be pretty important to you."

"It is, Johnnie. That man took something from me. He beat me, and when I found solace he...I am a very vengeful woman." She chuckled. "They say the most dangerous person in the world is a woman scorned."

"Then it ain't just the money you want."

"No. I want to hurt him the way he hurt me. But I want the money, too."

Two miles from town he reined his horse north into the foothills. By then the light was good enough that he picked up a trail that cut northeast and climbed steadily. They rode in silence. He let the horses take their time. That would get them to their destination

145

quicker than pushing them hard and having to stop now and then to let them blow. Where the cattle and horse trail petered out, they picked up a game trail and climbed through scrub oak, then into the lodgepole pines and ponderosas. Once, when they skirted the side of a hill, they saw two fat bucks below them. He recalled an uncle saying that the place to camp and graze a herd of cattle was wherever the antelope were the fattest. They were in Josh Bennett's country now, and the grass was still good. Brown, but high and waving in the breeze. Maybe he had pushed the cattle down too soon. Aw hell, who knows.

A warm sun bore down on them when they crossed open country, but in the shade the temperature was ten degrees cooler. They were in the shade of the trees most of the time. In places there was no trail at all, and John Wesley used a distant high snow-covered peak on their left as a landmark. His eyes were always picking out more landmarks.

At noon they stopped beside a stream where the horses could graze. She slid sorely down. "Ooh, my God. I'm used to riding, but not this far."

"I'll fix those stirrups for you. That'll make it a little easier." He opened two tins of dried beef and handed her one. While she ate he unlaced the stirrup leathers on Josh's saddle, took them up two holes and laced them again. He ate hurriedly and drank by lying on his belly beside the creek and putting his face in the water. She did the same, looking like a shapeless pile of clothes on the ground.

Two hours later they crossed the top of the pass. To the west the country rose sharply, and a hundred yards away the only trees were short, stunted, twisted pines. A quarter-mile farther west there were no trees at all, just huge granite boulders. Patches of snow still lay in the shady places. A cool wind whipped around their shoulders and sang in their ears. John Wesley's eyes watered in the wind, and Miss Mitchell pulled her head deeper inside the mackinaw. They rode on until they were under the top and in a sunny valley.

"Can we stop a minute, Johnnie?"

"Why? We're going downhill now and the horses are walking better."

"I can't tell you why. It's just that human animals have to have some privacy now and then."

"Oh, sure." He knew exactly what she was talking about and was relieved to hear her say it. When she disappeared behind a boulder he went into a grove of bare-limbed aspens.

Horseback again, she asked, "How much farther, Johnnie?"

Glancing at the sky, he said, "We'll be down there before dark. We're gonna come to a pretty good trail here in a little while. When we get down there it's only a mile or so to town. What do you plan on doing when we get there? We ought to let these horses rest a day before we go back."

"I'll have to go on ahead. We'll do the robbing tomorrow night."

Soon they were riding single file on a narrow trail and he had to turn in his saddle and look back at her. "I should have asked you before, but are you going back over the mountains with me?"

"Yes. In fact, I don't want to be seen in Rosebud while we're there."

"But you were there not long ago, weren't you? You went someplace."

"Not there. I went by stage to Durango where I met my friend. He traveled by rail. We finalized our plan then. Rosebud is a much bigger town than Cloudcroft, but still it's almost impossible to go around unrecognized."

"Yeah, I spent a night in Rosebud once."

"There are people who would recognize me and I intend to stay out of sight as much as possible."

"I should have asked you something else before. Exactly how are we going to do this?"

"I'll work out the details tonight with my friend."

"Then I won't know 'til the time comes."

"I'll inform you as soon as possible."

Yeah, he thought, you'll inform me about the robbery I'm gonna commit. You'll inform me when you get damned good and ready. In the meantime, I'm supposed to do as you say. I might turn out to be the biggest damn fool in the whole United States of America.

CHAPTER 21

Just before sundown they reined up on a rocky point and looked down on a wide tree-studded valley. The trees were all conifers. Scrub oak, red with rapidly falling leaves, grew thick in places. The railroad ran the length of the valley, and railroad pens and sidings sprawled across twenty acres just east of the busy town of Rosebud.

"We have to stay out of sight, Johnnie. Try to find a place where you can spend the night out of sight."

"No hotel for me, huh?"

"I'm afraid not. But you're accustomed to sleeping out."

"You know all about me, don't you?"

"Not everything, but enough."

Yeah, he thought grimly, she had asked around and knew something about him.

Looking downhill, he saw a small clearing among some of the scrub oak, and figured that would be as good a place as any to spend the night. He could hobble the horses and the mule there, and it was away from the trail. He headed in that direction, riding around boulders and through a stand of pine and spruce. Reining up in the clearing, he looked around and was satisfied with what he saw. They were surrounded by the buck brush. It was doubtful anyone would come through here.

"Now what?"

"I'll go on. My friend has a small house on this end of town and he has a stable and some hay. Your horse will be well-fed and rested."

"And that's where you'll spend the night."

"I can't go to a hotel. If you're worried about my virtue, don't. That would be a wasted worry."

"Is this Earl of Somethingorother gonna be in town?"

"Yes, unless he had a sudden change of plans. The trip to Denver is easy from here by rail car, and he travels back and forth."

"Uh-huh. If he had a change of plans so could everybody and everything else. We couldn't have come over these mountains for nothing, could we?"

"That's very unlikely. Whether the earl is here or not is immaterial. The money is here."

Dismounting, he started unloading the mule. "All light. I'll have to take your word for it. Can you find your way back to this spot?"

She took a long look at her surroundings. "There's that round boulder over there by the trail. Let's see, when I come from town to a place on the trail that is even with that rock, I can turn right and come straight to this spot. Will you watch for me?"

"I'll watch for you. When do you expect to be back?"

"By noon. Yes, I'll be back by noon and I'll have all the details."

"Yeah, all right."

He watched her ride away, pushing through the buck brush, and when she was out of sight he finished unsaddling the mule. He hobbled the mule, then unsaddled his horse and hobbled him. He'd eat out of a can that night. He had committed no crime yet and no one was looking for him, but just the same he'd rather not be seen.

While he lay in his blankets, covered by the tarp, he was comfortable, but he was thinking about her. Here he was sleeping alone, as always, while Valerie Mitchell was no doubt in bed with somebody else. She had come to his cabin twice, he had gone to her hotel room twice, he had brought her over the mountains, and now some other man, some dandy, was bedding her down.

Don't worry about her virtue, she had said. The best thing to do was to forget her. He wished he could forget her. If they were leaving together, going back over the mountains, would she stay in Cloudcroft for a while, maybe stay with him at the JB Ranch? Aw hell, she'd probably head for some big city where she could spend the money.

Aw hell.

The horse and mule were grazing peacefully when he got up at daylight. He led them to the nearest stream, a quarter-mile away, then opened a can of peaches. Blah. Cold. Tasteless. Boy, how he'd like to lope down to that town, park himself on a stool at a good cafe and stuff himself with some ham and eggs. Why the hell should he sit here and wait for some woman to come back and tell him what to do?

Well, one reason was that he was broke. He couldn't pay for a cafe meal. All he could do was depend on her.

She came back at noon. He was watching for her and saw her coming. No one else was in sight. Still wearing Josh Bennett's clothes, she stopped her horse on the trail, looked to her right and saw him watching her.

"It's all set," she said simply. "Tonight, as soon as it's dark."

She crawled out of the saddle and walked sorely over to his bedroll, then sat on it. "Johnnie, there has been one change of plans."

"Yeah?" Sure, he thought, sourly, there has to be a change of plans.

"My friend is going to do the robbing. There will be nothing for you to do but transport me back over these mountains. That's all you will have to do."

"Yeah?" He knew she had more to say and he waited.

"Of course, since my friend is doing all the robbing, taking all the risks, he doesn't want to divide the money evenly." She glanced his way to see how he was taking this, and went on, "He thinks you should be satisfied with two thousand dollars."

"Uh-huh. So all I have to do is wait here 'til the dirty work is done and see that you get back to Cloudcroft, and for that you'll pay me two thousand?"

"Well, that's not exactly right. You have to come down to the house with me. To the earl's house. The money will have to be carried on your pack mule. Besides, we'll have to leave town in the dark and I don't think I can find my way back here in the dark. Can you find our way?"

With a glance at the sky, he said, "If it's a clear night and there's any moon at all I can. And it looks like the sky is gonna stay clear."

"Good. It's all set then."

"Tell me something, Miss Mitchell, how is your friend gonna rob this gent? Stick a gun in his face?"

"Oh no, nothing like that. He wouldn't dare. No, he knows where the earl has his money hidden, and he'll just take it and hand it to us and go on about his business as if nothing has happened."

"Oh. Then the earl has his money hidden in his house instead of putting it in a bank. There has to be a bank down there. I remember seeing one."

"Yes, there is a bank. The Rosebud National Bank. But, uh, the earl has to have money handy, ready to, uh, pay off his hirelings. And he doesn't want anyone, not even the bankers, to know about his business dealings."

John Wesley was sitting on the ground, feet in front of him, knees up, and he studied the ground between his knees. "He's sure a shady character, this Earl Whataisname. How is your friend gonna steal the money without him knowing it?"

"He won't be at home."

"Oh, uh-huh. How does your friend know where the money is hidden?"

"He works for the earl. He knows."

"Did some spying on him, did he?"

"That's right. Did some spying."

He put his hands on the ground behind him and leaned back on them, gazed out over the buck brush. "Well, that's fine with me. I'm not greedy. There's two things I want to do on this trip, get some money, and put a stop to this earl's land-grabbing scheme. I hope we leave him so busted he'll have to bum a ride to England, or wherever he came from."

"I understand, Johnnie. You want to go back to your homestead and continue your way of living. Only, you want some money to rebuild your cabin and to buy whatever else you need."

"Uh-huh."

"And the Earl of Ravenshire is responsible for your cabin being destroyed, so it is only right that you should take some money from him."

"Uh-huh."

"You will get your wish. You'll get two thousand dollars, which should be more than enough to buy everything you need, and the earl won't succeed in his land scheme."

"Why not?"

"Because my friend knows all about it and has promised to inform on him."

"Why would he do that? It's nothing to him."

"Nothing financially, but, well, he promised me he would do it. I want him to."

"Uh-huh. Yeah, you said you're mad at this earl and want to get even. But if your friend spills the beans about his boss, won't he be in trouble?"

"I don't think so. He has a way. I don't know exactly what. Possibly, he will do it through someone else."

"Can I depend on him to do that?"

"The earl will be stopped." With that, Valerie Mitchell stood, stretched, and walked away into the brush.

John Wesley unsaddled the horse she had ridden and let him graze. Little was said the rest of the day. She was nervous, sitting, standing, pacing, sitting. He understood, and said nothing. The change in plans suited him just fine. He'd rather not point a gun at anybody anyway. This would be easier. Not as profitable, but profitable enough.

At sundown, he opened the last two tins of dried beef. He ate his, but she only nibbled at hers. He led the horses and the mule the quarter-mile to the creek, drank his fill of water, and let them drink. When he came back, he started saddling the animals.

"Be dark soon," he said. "Any special time?"

"No. Just so it's dark." She was standing, hugging herself and rocking on her toes with nervousness.

Glancing at the sky again, he allowed, "There's some clouds moving in from the west, but I don't think they'll hide the moon, and it's a half-moon. We'll be seen."

"Men on horseback are on the streets of Rosebud all the time. Just as long as we're not recognized."

"There's some lights coming on down there. Rosebud has street lamps on some of the corners, as I recall."

"Yes. But on only a few of the corners. We won't be close to any of them."

"That's good. I don't care to be seen either."

She picked up the reins of the horse she had ridden and mounted without any help. She could handle a horse. Learned on a farm in Illinois, she'd said. A farm girl. Didn't look like a farm girl, but she could talk like one. Or maybe she was a town girl. Town kids liked to ride. Some town kids were as crazy about horses as the ranch and farm kids. She didn't know the mountains, but she wasn't helpless. Could make a ranch wife if she wanted to.

They rode silently. He didn't know what was going on in her mind, but it was plain to see she was nervous and maybe a little scared. Himself? Not as nervous as he was before she announced the new plan. So he was going to help rob a rich man. He had nothing against the rich—unless they used their wealth and influence to take an unfair advantage of some working stiff. He knew at least one rich man who had done that. To him.

While they were riding silently in the dark, it all came back, and it helped ease his conscience about robbing this Earl Whatever.

It was on the Turkey Track. He was sacking out a wild colt in a corral. His method was to tie the colt's right hind foot up, just a little. Just pull it forward enough that the colt could touch the ground with its toe, but couldn't step down. That way, the colt couldn't kick or buck but could move around, although moving was hard work. It usually took only a few minutes for the colt to realize it wasn't being hurt and it was easier to stand still. At that point, John Wesley rubbed the colt all over with a feed sack, climbed up on its back and got it used to being handled. Only trouble was, some of the colts fought so hard they threw themselves and then refused to get up until they got their wind. That's what was happening when the rich son of a bitch came along. John Wesley was in no hurry. The colt would get up when it felt like it, and it would be a little gentler when it did. He hunkered down against the corral and waited.

"Hey. What are you doing to that horse?"

Looking up from under his hat brim, John Wesley saw the man coming through the corral gate, stupidly leaving it open. He and two of his compadres had showed up two days earlier, saying they wanted to visit the ranch in which they had a financial interest.

"I ask you something, cowpuncher, and I want an answer." He was big but soft looking, in his lowcut shoes, wool pants with a crease down the front, and white shirt. His head was bare, and the breeze was standing most of his thin hair on end.

"Why, uh..." John Wesley stood and didn't know what to say.

"Why is that horse laying down?"

"Oh, uh, he's just, uh..."

"Let him up. Let him up this instant." The big soft man was standing right in front of John Wesley, glaring at him, face red.

"Well, uh, he can get up whenever he wants to." He'd never spoken to a rich Easterner before. Should he say "Sir," or something?

"I want no arguments from the hired help. When I tell you to do something you do it immediately."

"Well, uh..."

He was standing closer now, so close that John Wesley could smell his breath. "Don't argue with me. I am not accustomed to having my orders ignored by some stupid cowpoke."

Now this was getting serious. Maybe back East men could insult each other without a fight, but not in the West. The big man's face was getting red, and so was John Wesley's.

"Move, you oaf. Do as I say or I'll fire you so fast you won't know what happened to you."

"Sir, it's like I said, he can—" He didn't get to finish what he was about to say.

"Look here, you ignorant country bumpkin, when I—" he didn't get to finish what he was about to say either.

WHOP. Without thinking, John Wesley bailed his right hand and brought it up from his waist. It connected squarely with the big man's nose. John Wesley had both fists up, ready for a fight. He and his cousins were always fighting. Punching and getting punched was nothing new to him. But that was the end of this fight.

The big man sat down hard on the seat of his pants and grabbed his nose with both hands. Blood poured between his fingers and ran down onto his white shirt. He blubbered something that John Wesley didn't understand.

With a feeling of disgust at how easily the man had given up,

John Wesley untied the colt and got it to stand. Not knowing what else to do he went to the bunkhouse, sat on his bunk a while, then went out and started repairing a broken halter. When he looked at the corral, he saw the big man was gone.

He was at supper in the cookshack that night when the sheriff showed up and told him he was under arrest.

Many times while he rotted in jail he wished there were a way to get even with that rich Eastern son of a bitch. There was no way.

"We're almost there," the girl said, finally. "There's a light in the corner room. He's ready for us."

CHAPTER 22

The half-moon was showing itself in the western sky and putting out barely enough light that they could see the back side of a big two-story house on the edge of town. There was no corral or stable behind the house. With a railroad for transportation, the earl probably didn't want anything to do with horses.

"Wait here," the girl whispered. "I'll go in and get the money."

She dismounted and handed him her reins. He sat his saddle and waited. The back door opened when she stepped up onto a small porch and knocked lightly. A young man looked out. He had a handlebar moustache and thick dark hair with long sideburns. She went in, and came out again.

"Johnnie," she said in a half-whisper. "We need you in here a minute."

"You need me?" he whispered. "Why?"

"We need your help. Will you come in here please?"

This wasn't what he expected. He was supposed to do no more than load the money on his mule and lead the way back over the mountains to Cloudcroft. But before he could argue she went inside again, leaving the door open a crack. Only a dim light came through the door. Reluctantly, he got down and tied the animals to a rail fence. With a little fear, wishing he were somewhere else, he went to the door, opened it wide enough to step through.

"In here, Johnnie." She was standing in a hall, near an open door, beckoning.

He had to cross a kitchen to go to her, walking quietly. The young man, in a striped shirt and wool pants, stood beside her.

"In here."

At the door he stopped and looked through. It was a bedroom, with a big chiffonier, an oak wardrobe as high as the ceiling, and a brass bedstead. A man lay on the bed. A fat middle-aged man.

"Johnnie, meet the Earl of Ravenshire."

The light from the hall barely illuminated the bedroom, but John Wesley didn't need to see better. The man lay still. A bright spot of blood stained his shirt, high on the left side. He was dead.

"Oh no," John Wesley said, backing out of the doorway. "No. This wasn't in the plan."

She quickly stepped in front of him. "It was an accident, Johnnie. William didn't plan to do it this way. He came home when he wasn't supposed to."

"It doesn't matter. It's murder. I'm getting out of here."

"Wait, Johnnie. It's all right. He won't be missed for several days. The money is right here. All we have to do is dispose of the body."

"We? Not me. No ma'am."

"It'll be easy, Johnnie. William knows of an abandoned mine shaft only a few miles from town. The body won't be found there."

"Who? William?"

"Yes. Meet William Lisecki. He's a clerk at the bank." Suddenly Valerie Mitchell clamped her mouth shut and turned away.

The young man spoke, hissed through his teeth, "You fool. You damned fool." He turned to John Wesley. "What she means is I am a clerk for the Earl of Ravenshire. I knew where he had the money hidden. I didn't mean to kill him, but he surprised me. He came up behind me when I was counting the money. I—"

"There's a house right over there," John Wesley said. "The neighbor must have heard the shot. It's time to get out of here." He started to push past William Lisecki.

"No. There was no shot. I, uh, I used a knife. No one is the wiser."

Shaking his head, John Wesley said, "No. No sir. This is no place for me." To Valerie Mitchell he said, "I promised to take you back to Cloudcroft. If you still want to go, let's get started."

"Listen," Lisecki hurried to a position in front of John Wesley, "I can do you a favor. I knew about the land scheme. I can provide documents to prove fraud."

It was enough to make John Wesley pause. "Yeah, that's what Miss Mitchell told me."

"She told you correctly."

"So you overheard this gent's conversation about it."

"That's true."

"Where?"

"At the, uh, here in this house."

"You've spent a lot of time here, is that it?"

"Yes I have."

"Would you recognize the sheriff from Cloudcroft?"

"Of course. I've seen Sheriff Watkins several times. He and Mr., uh, the earl, conferred quite often."

"Was the sheriff being paid by the earl?" John Wesley had a strong urge to get out of the house and get far away, but he also wanted to confirm his suspicion about Sheriff Joseph Watkins.

"He was borrowing money to, uh—" Then the young man clamped his mouth shut and turned away.

John Wesley pondered that. He put his head down and frowned at the wooden floor, turning it over in his mind. When he looked up he was looking into the bore of a gun.

"Don't move," William Lisecki barked. "Move one inch before I tell you to and we'll have two bodies to dispose of."

John Wesley noticed that the young man's shirt was loose enough to hide a gun. That must be where he had it.

"The time has come to do something," Lisecki said. "We need your help, cowboy, and we are going to get it."

The young man was nervous. His finger on the trigger of a late model Colt .44 was twitching. The gun was shoved against John Wesley's stomach. John Wesley didn't move while his own Colt .44 was lifted out of its holster.

The girl spoke in a high, thin whisper, "What are you going to do, William?"

"I'm going to shoot this cowboy if he doesn't pick up that body

158

and put it on his pack horse."

"You can't do that. We...I...need him."

Holding two guns now, the young man backed up a few steps, cocked his head to one side and frowned. Then he said, "Perhaps...perhaps we don't need him."

"What do you mean, William?"

"Look at it this way. Suppose this cowboy came here to rob Mr., uh, the Earl of Ravenshire, and the earl surprised him in the act. He didn't want to shoot and alert the neighbors so he stabbed the earl. I came along and shot the robber. Yeah, we could work it that way."

"What about the money?"

"Oh, we'd have to leave some of it, enough to make it look like this cowboy had it in his hands when he was surprised. But there's plenty of money there." His eyes went to two leather satchels on the floor near his feet.

"But I have to get away. I can't find my way back to Cloudcroft, and if I take the train anywhere I'll be recognized and I can't allow that to happen."

"Hmm." That stumped him. He frowned at the floor a long moment. John Wesley had his eyes on the guns in Lisecki's hands. He gathered his muscles and was ready to jump and grab for both guns. Lisecki looked up and raised the pistol in his right hand. "Don't move. I can kill you and make myself a hero doing it."

John Wesley believed him and stood still.

The girl said, "We'll have to go ahead with our original plan, Will."

"No, we'll hide you."

"I can't stay in hiding long enough."

"Listen, our original plan is ruined. I didn't want to kill him, but I had to do it. Now we have to change our plan."

"We can get rid of the body."

"Perhaps. But eventually his body will be found and then people will start asking questions." Lisecki cocked his head to one side again, thinking. "No, I like my new plan better. We'll get you out of town someway."

"There is no other way. We've talked about this before." Her voice took on a pleading note. "I have to go back to Cloudcroft and take a stage from there."

He was still thinking, then, "No. I'm sorry, Ellen, but we have to change our plan."

"Oh no." She was no longer pleading. She had gathered some resolve. "Were it not for me, you wouldn't have known where the money was. You'd always be a clerk in a..." She caught herself, and added, "This was my idea and we're going to do it my way."

A sneer turned up one side of Lisecki's mouth. "Your idea, yes, but you couldn't do it without my help. And you just had to bring in this cowboy."

"That was the only way it would work. I can't use public transportation. I had to stay away."

John Wesley looked from one to the other. Somehow he wasn't afraid. But he was damned interested.

Lisecki said, "And now you're back, Ellen. And why did you come back? To rob your husband. Hmm." He was thinking again. "So what if I came along and spoiled your little scheme. Yeah, you persuaded this cowboy to help you rob him, and I came along and caught you in the act." He took aim at John Wesley's chest.

"Will." She was pleading again. "You can't do this. I told you I didn't want anyone killed. We were going to just steal from a thief. Now you've already killed my husband and...no, you can't do this. You can't leave me to take the..." Sudden understanding brought a horrified expression to her face. "Oh no. You can't do this."

"Sorry, Ellen. A fellow has to look out for himself. You were good in bed and I surely enjoyed it, but that's all you were ever good for." His finger tightened on the trigger.

She screamed, "Will," and she jumped at him desperately clawing at him.

The Colt .44 in his right hand popped. The racket filled the hall and echoed throughout the house.

Valerie Mitchell—Ellen—slumped to the floor. Her last words were, "Will...oh Will."

For a few seconds, John Wesley was stunned. It took that long for his mind to believe what he'd seen. Without hesitation, he'd shot and killed her. Every muscle in John Wesley's body tensed. His mind screamed, GET HIM.

The bore of the .44 came up. John Wesley could see into the bore. In his mind's eye he could see the bullet that was going to kill him. The girl's body was between him and the dandy. There was no way to avoid it. He froze, waiting for it.

William Lisecki's finger tightened on the trigger. He paused. He stepped back a step and kicked one of the two satchels toward John Wesley. It slid on the wooden floor and stopped against the girl's body.

"Pick it up."

"What?" John Wesley was puzzled.

"I said pick it up."

"Why?"

"Don't ask questions, just do it. I can kill you anyway."

Now he knew why. The dandy wanted it to look like John Wesley had stabbed the earl and shot the girl and was on his way down the hall with the money in his hand when the hero came in and shot him. Or did the dandy want to make it look like he himself had shot the girl? Maybe put the knife in the girl's hand so it would appear that she had stabbed her husband and was about to stab him.

Her husband?

"Do it, goddam it. Right now."

He had to reach over the girl's body to get hold of the satchel. William Lisecki stepped back to where John Wesley couldn't even hope to jump at him. Bending, John Wesley picked up the satchel by its leather handle. Could he throw it at Lisecki? Could he do anything? Anything was better than nothing.

The dandy's finger tightened on the trigger again. A cruel smile came over his face. "This is going to be perfect." He chuckled. "The perfect crime."

Do something. Anything. John Wesley eyed the gun, muscles bunched. Then he saw movement behind the dandy. A man appeared from the kitchen, walking softly, a gun in his hand.

Sheriff Joseph Watkins barked, "Hold it right there."

CHAPTER 23

William Lisecki froze. John Wesley froze. Sheriff Joseph Watkins stood spraddle-legged, a six-gun in his hand pointed at Lisecki's back. He wore a brown hat now, not one that John Wesley had seen before, and he had on a heavy duck jacket that covered his badge. "Drop those guns," he ordered.

Lisecki let the two six-guns slide from his fingers. The one that fell from his right hand was cocked, and it fired when it hit the floor. The bullet slammed into the wall, floor level.

John Wesley started to pick up his own gun. "Don't move," the sheriff barked. His gun was aimed at John Wesley now.

"What? Why? He was about to shoot me."

"Yeah, so I see."

"Well, what...?"

"Shut up and don't move. Not 'til I figure this out."

"I can tell you what happened."

"All right, talk."

Glancing at Lisecki, down at the dead girl, back at the sheriff, John Wesley said, "There's a dead man in there on a bed. He's been stabbed."

"Who?"

"I think he's the Earl of Raven-something-or-other."

"Who?" The sheriff s eyes narrowed.

"Well, go look."

"Don't move. Don't either of you move. Don't move your

hands, feet, eyeballs or anything." Sheriff Watkins kept his eyes on John Wesley and the dandy as he sidled past them, his back to the wall. At the bedroom door, his eyes took in the dead man, then jerked back to the two men in the hallway. "Who killed him?"

"He did," John Wesley answered.

Lisecki said quickly, "That's a lie, sheriff. I came here to see Mr. Rischling about something and I found these two. His wife tried to stab me and I shot her. I was going to turn this man over to the law when you came in."

"What's in the suitcases?"

"I don't know. I haven't had a chance to look, but I'll bet it's money."

"Money, huh?" Watkins pushed one of the bags with his toe, then, keeping his eyes on the two men, squatted and fumbled the latch open with his left hand. He took a quick look inside, then another longer look. "Why, that son of a bitch."

Straightening, the sheriff frowned at the two men, down at the dead girl, and back. No one spoke. Sheriff Watkins's eyebrows pulled together as he pondered what he'd seen and heard.

Finally, he asked, "His wife, you said? I didn't know he had a wife."

"Yes sir. She left him last spring, but I think they're still married."

Squinting at Lisecki, Watkins said, "I've seen you before somewhere."

"Yes sir, in the bank. I saw you talking to Mr. Rischling, and I remember you as a sheriff from Cloudcroft."

"Oh." He squinted next at John Wesley. "Budeen, what the hell're you doin' here?"

"I came with her."

"Why?"

He couldn't answer. What could he say? What lie could he tell? Lisecki answered:

"They came here to rob him, that's obvious. Kill him and rob him."

"And you just happened to walk in at the right time, huh?"

"Yes sir. I happened to have a pistol with me and when she

attacked me with a knife I shot her."

"Where's the knife?"

"Oh, it's, uh, I, uh, she dropped it in the bedroom."

"And you shot her out here in the hall."

"Yes sir."

"You're a liar." Turning his eyes to John Wesley, he said, "Budeen, tell me what the hell is going on here or I'll drop both of you."

"But sir, you can't just shoot us down." Now the dandy was pleading. "You're a sworn officer of the law."

"Oh yes, I can." His eyebrows pulled together again. "Matter of fact, that's a good idea." A slow smile spread across his face. "That's a fine idea." He chuckled. "Who says there's no such thing as luck. Here I was, comin' to see Old Owen about another loan, and I no more than get to the back door when I near a shot. I don't just run in and get shot at, I come in quiet, careful. And what do I find?"

He didn't need to finish, but he did anyway. "I find three people, includin' his own wife, robbin' him." The sheriff s eyes went again to the satchels. "I'll bet there's a lot of money there." Chuckling again, he added, "Yes sir. I'll bet there's enough that I could leave some and still have enough to do anything I wantta do."

A groan came out of John Wesley. He'd heard this scheme before. Very recently.

Lisecki pleaded, "But sheriff, you can't just shoot us. You represent the law." He was holding his hands out in front of him in a pleading gesture. He took a step toward the sheriff. "Please, you can't do this. You can't get away with it. You can't..."

The sheriff shot him. Shot him squarely in the center of the chest and watched him fall. He had to step back a step to keep the man from falling on his boots.

John Wesley wasn't stunned this time. He had his wits about him. But he didn't get a chance to do anything. The sheriff immediately thumbed the hammer back on his six-gun and pointed it squarely at the center of John Wesley's chest.

"Too bad about you, Budeen. I was hoping you'd just leave the country and not get killed, but you had to go and get hooked up with this woman here. If it wasn't for her you'd have high-tailed it when your cabin burned down. Or sold out cheap. But no, you had to listen to her."

For the second time in ten minutes, John Wesley looked into the bore of a gun and saw death coming. Again, it was desperation time. He had no chance at all, but he had to try.

The dandy on the floor groaned a long, pitiful groan, and tried to sit up, got halfway up. Blood covered the front of his shirt, and his heart was still pumping blood. He tried to talk, but only another groan came out. Sheriff Watkins pointed the six-gun at the top of his head, and took his eyes off John Wesley for a moment.

John Wesley was on him, had one hand around his right wrist, the other hand around the gun barrel, then both hands on the gun. The sheriff jerked his arm, twisted, tried to knock his assailant away with his left shoulder. John Wesley hung on, hung on for his life, butted the sheriff in the face with his head. His hat fell off. He got his right hip against the sheriff and tried to swing him over his hip. Still, the sheriff kept his hold on the gun. John Wesley butted him again.

The two men fought, each knowing he was fighting for his life. Straining, grunting, cursing, they fought.

John Wesley tried again to yank the sheriff over his right hip, and succeeded. The sheriff hit the floor on his back, but held onto the gun. John Wesley dropped onto him, one knee in his crotch. A yelp of pain came from the sheriff. Still he held onto the gun. John Wesley had both knees on him now, one in his crotch and the other on his stomach. He bounced, hitting the sheriff hard with both knees. A loud grunt. Again.

The sheriff was weakening. He bounced again, pounding the sheriff low on the stomach with his left knee. Then he twisted half-around and got his right knee on the sheriff's throat, then pounded with that knee.

The gun came free. John Wesley had it in his hands.

Sitting astraddle the sheriff now, John Wesley put the bore of the gun against the sheriff s nose. He stayed in that position for a long moment. Neither man moved.

The fight was over.

Finally, without speaking, John Wesley got to his feet. He was breathing hard. The sheriff s nose was bloody, and his mouth was open, gulping in air. For another long moment, they stayed where they were. Then John Wesley reached down for his gun that was on the floor near the sheriff s boots. He put it in its holster, and, still holding the sheriff s six-shooter, picked up Lisecki's late model gun, shifted it to his right hand and cocked the hammer. He put the sheriff's gun in his belt.

Lisecki was on his back now, lying still. The hole in his chest was no longer spouting blood.

With three guns in his possession, John Wesley looked around. Two people were dead on the floor.

The sheriff picked himself up, bending low with pain, "What are you gonna do, Budeen?"

Do? He didn't know what to do. He tried to think of what to do.

"There's enough money there for both of us, Budeen." Sheriff Joseph Watkins dragged a shirt sleeve across his nose. The sleeve was bloody.

"Yeah, uh." He had to think this out.

"We can get away easy. Those horses out there, they have to be yours."

"Yeah."

"I came around the long way, by train, but I'm not well-known in Rosebud. Nobody recognized me."

"Well, uh, there's neighbors around here. Somebody heard the shots."

"No. Not likely. I was just outside the back door when a shot was fired, and I barely heard it. These walls are thick, built that way to keep out the cold." When John Wesley said nothing, he talked on, "The nearest neighbor is a good hundred yards east. He didn't hear anything. We can get away."

"No, uh..." What John Wesley wanted was to get out of the house and get started back over the mountains. But what was he going to do with the sheriff? He couldn't leave him here with the money, and he couldn't turn him over to the Rosebud lawmen. If he did he'd have to answer some questions that would be hard to answer.

The sheriff read his mind. "Either we leave here together, Budeen, or I go back to my plan. You know, make it look like I walked in on a robbery." He watched John Wesley's face, then said,

"If you don't want a share of the money, then just go. Git long gone. I won't let on that I saw you here. How's that?"

Shaking his head, John Wesley tried to think. What was the best thing to do? Maybe Sheriff Watkins was right. Just go. The sheriff would steal the money, most of it, but what did he care? With the money, and with John Wesley knowing all about him, Joseph Watkins would head for parts unknown and that would put a stop to the land grab in the Turquoise Basin.

But no, he couldn't let him get by with it. This man here knew all about Josh Bennett's murder. If he didn't have anything to do with it himself, he at least knew who did. He was responsible for the killing of the Jenkinses. And he had a hand in burning down John Wesley's cabin.

"Tell you what, Budeen, you take some of the money with you. Nobody will know. You can use it to build a new cabin or hell, you can use it for a lot of things. What do you say?"

John Wesley didn't answer. What to do? What the hell to do?

Sheriff Joseph Watkins made the decision for him.

Moving fast for a paunchy man, fast and strong, he had his arms around John Wesley's waist, pinning his arms at his sides. The sheriff's arms were like steel bands, squeezing. He used one of John Wesley's tricks and butted his opponent in the face with his head. John Wesley felt his teeth rattle, his arms growing numb. He tried to knee the paunchy man, couldn't. He tried bending his knees then jumping up. The sheriff held on. He tried to wrestle his gun hand free. He couldn't move.

Using his forehead like a club, Sheriff Watkins butted his opponent again, squeezed with all his strength. John Wesley couldn't breath. His strength was going fast. He concentrated on moving his gun hand. Could move it only a little. He jerked the trigger of the .44, trying to shoot the sheriff in the foot. The slug buried itself in the floor. He tried again. Missed again. He was afraid to fire a third shot. He could shoot himself. He tried for the second time to bend his knees and get under the sheriff's arm. The arms slipped up an inch.

Then he let his knees go slack, let them collapse, and he slipped down onto his back. The sheriff came down with him, on top of him, but his hold loosened. John Wesley got his right hand free. He put the bore of the gun against the sheriff's chest.

He pulled the trigger.

The gunshot echoed through the house. John Wesley had a dead weight on top of him. Grunting, he rolled the man off and stood. His lungs were pumping air, and he felt weak, shaky. Three dead bodies were on the floor in the hall, and another was on a bed in the bedroom. Four dead people. He was the only one alive. He'd wrestled with Sheriff Joseph Watkins twice and won both times. It took a moment for him to realize he was alive while everyone else was dead. Valerie Mitchell, shot. Her ex-lover William Lisecki, shot. Sheriff Joseph Watkins, shot. He looked down at himself. A small spot of blood was on his shirt. He touched himself at that spot. He wasn't hurt. It was the sheriff's blood.

He realized he was holding Lisecki's gun, and he dropped it near Lisecki's body. He had the sheriff s gun, another .44, in his belt. He jerked it free and dropped it beside the sheriff. It occurred to him that—as far as anyone could tell—the sheriff and Lisecki had fought it out and shot each other. The sheriff had shot first, but Lisecki had lived long enough to get in a shot, too.

Still feeling weak, he picked up his hat and put it on. He started toward the kitchen, then stopped.

Two satchels of money were at his feet. A lot of money. More money than he'd ever seen, ever dreamed of having. Stolen money. It was his for the taking. All he had to do was put a satchel in each of the panniers on his pack mule and ride away.

"Huh," he grunted. His mouth turned down in a grimace. The perfect crime, someone had said recently. He could do as Lisecki planned, as the sheriff planned, take most of the money, but not all, and nobody would know. Nobody would know how much money the earl had stolen, and nobody would know that most of it was missing. As far as anybody knew, John Wesley Budeen had never been here. Nobody alive, that is.

Take it, John Wesley. Take it and run, you fool.

Four people were dead because of that money.

"Naw." Then with long quick steps he went through the kitchen and out the back door.

He hoped it wasn't too late to get the hell out of there.

CHAPTER 24

He rode at a walk, not wanting hoofbeats to attract attention, leading a pack mule and a horse carrying Josh Bennett's saddle. The half-moon put out enough light that he could see the road out of town. A mile out he quit the road and turned south, looking for the trail that came out of the mountains. Then the moon went behind a cloud and he couldn't see the trail. Riding parallel with the road and about a mile south of it, he knew he had passed the trail in the dark. He turned the horses around and went back, straining his eyes, wishing the moon would come out again. Crossing a narrow gulley, he remembered that the trail was beside the gulley, and he turned his horses south and into the buck brush. Nope. The brush was too thick. This was not the place. Turning again, he continued back toward town, crossed another gulley. Rode into the brush again. Nope.

Dammit, was he going to have to wait until daylight to find his way over the mountains? He couldn't wait. Like Valerie Mitchell, or Ellen, or whatever the hell her name was, he didn't want to be seen.

The night sky was overcast now. There was little chance the moon would come out again. Turning back away from town he rode. If he could find a way into those hills at all he could spend the night out of sight of Rosebud, then go on in the morning. Riding over the mountains in the dark wasn't his favorite pastime anyway. Another gulley, this one shallower than the others. Hell, the foothills were full of gulleys created by snowmelt running downhill. Reining his horse uphill, he found the brush wasn't so thick. He could ride through it

169

here. Maybe he was finally on the trail.

Climbing steadily now, he still wasn't sure he was on the trail he wanted to be on, but he was going in the right direction. He'd keep going until he ran into a cliff or a pile of boulders he couldn't get over, or until he was dragged off his horse by tree limbs or buck brush. A couple of miles farther a huge round boulder loomed up to his right, and he believed it was the one Valerie Mitchell had picked out as a landmark. He hoped it was.

"Come on, old ponies," he said aloud, "let's keep going. Let's get home."

Now that he had reason to believe he was on the trail, he began to think about how foolish he'd been. Just plain stupid. He'd allowed a young woman to talk him into a sorry mess that ended with four people killed. It was supposed to be a simple robbery. All he had to do was stick a gun in somebody's face, take a pile of money and disappear into the dark mountains. Maybe that's the way she had it planned. Told her lover she didn't want anybody killed. Her lover?

"Yep. No doubt about that. She'd been sneaking around behind her husband's back."

Her husband?

That's what Lisecki had said. That dead man in the bedroom was her husband. She was married to the Earl of Ravenshire. Or was she?

Still climbing, horses breathing hard, he left Rosebud behind. At a small clearing on a ridge, John Wesley reined up to let the horses blow. From there he could look back and see the dim lights of the town. The wind was picking up and stirring the treetops. Something wet hit him in the face. Snow.

The sky was black now, no moon, no stars. The country ahead of him was black. If he went on he could get lost. Stay here, he said to himself. Roll up in those blankets and that tarp and wait out the night. Another snow flake pelted him in the face.

"Dammit," he muttered, "just what I need." A heavy snow could keep him from going over the mountains. A light snow could be dangerous too. If it snowed only a short time and quit, he'd leave tracks that would be easy to follow. He could only hope he was high enough and far enough from town that nobody would come across his tracks. Go on, he said to himself. Go as far as you can. He touched spurs to his horse and went on.

Pulling his head as far into the collar of his mackinaw as he could, he puzzled over what had happened back there in Rosebud. Nothing turned out the way it was supposed to. Nobody was who he or she was supposed to be. The young woman's friend was her ex-lover. He wasn't a bookkeeper, he was a clerk in a bank. That's what she'd said. Come to think of it, she'd clammed up when she said it as if she'd let something slip. And later, she told the young man—William Lisecki was his name—he'd be nothing but a clerk if it weren't for her. The whole thing was her idea. She knew where the money was hidden.

Yeah, if she lived with this earl, she'd sooner or later find his hidey hole. She'd become suspicious. And he got careless. When he thought she was in bed or taking a bath or something, he went to his stash. She'd peeked and seen it. He was a thief, she'd said. Did he steal the money? From where did he steal it?

The horses were climbing, and he hadn't been hit by a tree limb and they hadn't come to anything they couldn't climb. They were on a trail, and there was only one trail in the Blue Range. Horses had good night vision, and his saddle horse was instinctively following a trail.

More snowflakes hit him in the face. Wet snow, the kind that sticks. He pulled his hat down tighter and ducked his head. Hell, he might as well keep his head down, he couldn't see where they were going anyway.

"Keep walking, feller," he said to the horse.

Sheriff Joseph Watkins had said he went to Rosebud to borrow money from "Old Owen." That had to be the dead man on the bed.

"Aw for crying out loud," John Wesley said to himself. "How dumb can a man get?"

The dead man was no English earl. That was just a made-up story. He was a banker of some kind. An officer in the Rosebud bank. Hell yes. William Lisecki was a clerk in the bank. He'd seen the sheriff there and overheard some of his conversation with Owen Somethingorother. Mr. Rischling, Lisecki had called him. Lisecki knew about the land scheme from overhearing the conversation. The dead man on the bed was Owen Rischling, and he and the sheriff were the ones who schemed to own all of the Turquoise Basin.

And Owen Rischling was a thief himself. His wife was wise to him. He was stealing from the bank.

John Wesley spoke aloud, "Well, I'll be damned. And I thought I was doing something dishonest. Hell, every damned body is a thief."

Snow was coming down steadily now, and the small wet flakes had turned to big fat ones. The horse carrying an empty saddle was tied to the crossbuck saddle on the mule and John Wesley was leading the mule. They were strung out single file. The ground was rapidly being covered with snow. But John Wesley was lost in thought.

This Owen Rischling was stealing from the bank. A little at a time. And keeping it at his house where he could put it back right quick if anybody got suspicious. When he got enough money together, he'd leave the country, go to South America maybe.

But if Owen Rischling was planning to head for South America with stolen money, he had no use for land in Colorado.

The land scheme was the sheriff's idea and nobody else's. Sheriff Watkins was borrowing money from the bank to buy title to the homesteads and to pay off some gun hands. He might have been slipping the bank officer a little extra cash to make borrowing easy, but Old Watkins and Mr. Rischling were going separate ways.

And Rischling, while he was putting together a big enough stash, had married a pretty young blond. Yeah, he liked the good life. He liked young women.

It might have worked if the young woman had been faithful, and if he'd kept his secret from her. But no, he was mean to her, beat her, she'd said, and she'd found solace, as she put it, with another man. A clerk at the bank. Old Owen got wise and threw her out. He didn't divorce her, just gave her a few bucks and sent her down the road. Told everybody she had gone to visit her family somewhere. He figured that by the time his friends and neighbors began to wonder when she was coming back, he'd have his pile and be gone.

The horse was beginning to wander. Instead of going uphill, it wanted to turn and go back downhill. John Wesley guessed they had come to where the trail petered out. With nothing to follow the horse was trying to take an easy route. He wished he could see. He knew where the trail petered out, and if that was where they were, he knew how much farther they had to go to get to the top of the pass. But now the snow had covered the ground, and even if he had the night vision of a horse he couldn't see the trail. Or the lack of a trail. He reined up, trying to decide what to do.

The snow was still coming down and the wind was getting stronger. His ears were numb from the cold wind. Ought to find a windbreak somewhere and hole up until the storm blows over, he thought. Hell, he couldn't see a windbreak if one was right in front of him.

Men have died in these hills. Froze to death. He ought to hole up.

No, that wouldn't be smart either. If it keeps on snowing like this, he wouldn't be able to get over the pass and down the other side. He could be snowed in up here.

He spoke aloud again, "Sorry, fellers, we've got to get home. Keep going." He turned his horse uphill and touched its sides with his spurs. The animal obeyed, and they were climbing again. When the horse's front feet dropped into a gulley, he knew they had lost their way. It was a hard struggle getting out of the gulley, but scrambling, forefeet pawing for a foothold, the horse got them out. John Wesley reined up and let the horse catch its wind. He dismounted, and groped his way back to the horse carrying an empty saddle.

Working by feel, he untied that horse from the mule's crossbuck saddle, tied his horse there in its place and mounted the spare horse. Now he wished he hadn't shortened the stirrup leathers to suit Valerie Mitchell, but he could ride that way. His knees would cramp, but he could ride. Heading uphill again, he spoke to the animals, "Don't quit on me, fellers. Keep going and we'll get home." He got them moving again.

Valerie Mitchell? No. Her name was Ellen. She'd even lied to him about her name. Ellen Somethingorother. Mrs. Rischling. Married, but separated. Went back to Denver or wherever Old Owen had found her, and brooded. Got to thinking about her husband's thievery and the money he had hidden in the house. Decided to try to get it.

Finding some help was no problem. Her lover boy. She wrote him a letter or sent him a telegraph or something. She spelled it all out for him. Well, no, not all out. For some reason or other she didn't trust him enough to tell him where the money was stashed. He wouldn't know that until she came back to Rosebud and showed him. That way she'd be sure to get her share.

Only she couldn't go back to Rosebud. She'd be recognized. And if her husband knew she was in town at the same time his stash disappeared, he'd know who to look for. And if the Rosebud lawdogs knew she was in town the same time her husband disappeared or was found murdered, they'd sure want to ask her some hard questions.

So she couldn't be seen. Couldn't travel by railroad or stage or anything else. She had to walk or ride a horse. She had to get there in the dark and stay in the dark.

His fresh horse didn't want to climb hills either, and he had to be constantly reining it back. At least they were in the open now where he wouldn't get knocked off his horse by a tree limb. He remembered an open park near the top of the pass, which meant they were either going in the right direction or were far away from where he wanted to be.

He would have given half of what he owned to know which.

Owned? Hell, he didn't even have a place to sleep. Had a few cattle and horses, and had a three-sided shelter and a stack of hay for them, but nothing for himself. No money, no nothing. Should have taken some of that money back there. Naw. That money was bloody. It was bad luck.

Sure was bad luck for Valerie Mitchell—Ellen. John Wesley believed she really didn't want her husband killed. All she wanted was the money, and maybe to get even with him for mistreating her and throwing her out. It was something that ate on her until she had to cook up a plan to get it. She'd asked and found out that a range of mountains separated the towns of Rosebud and Cloudcroft. There had to be a way over those mountains. If there was, she could travel over the mountains on a horse and get into her husband's house at night without being seen.

She could ride a horse. But she didn't know the way from one town to the other, and she didn't want to make the trip alone. So, instead of dividing the money two ways, she had to cut in somebody else. Somebody who knew the mountains and had horses. She'd traveled by stage to Cloudcroft and started looking. Luck was with her. She found John Wesley Budeen.

Everything worked just right for her. It only took a few questions to learn that John Wesley was brought up a rawhider, and the rawhiders were a shady bunch who wouldn't pass up a chance at some easy money, law or no law.

Now, all she had to do was make some final plans with her ex-lover and persuade John Wesley to take part. Luck was with her there, too. She got together with this William Lisecki somewhere. She was gone the first time John Wesley went to see her at her hotel. Probably took a stage to Durango or someplace where she could meet Lisecki. That was when he told her about Sheriff Joseph Watkins's plan to own the whole Turquoise Basin. Or, no, the first time they met he came to her at Cloudcroft. Yeah, the hotel clerk said she'd had a man visitor, and the next time they met it was somewhere else.

Anyway, Lisecki knew about the sheriff and what a crook he was, and he overheard him say someone had to die before he could get the three pieces of the Basin that were already claimed. He was a listener, this Lisecki, and a schemer. He figured his big ears would come in handy one day. What he'd learned about the sheriff at Cloudcroft was just what his lady friend needed to persuade John Wesley to help her.

His feet were so cold in the stirrups that he had to get down and walk a while to get the blood circulating. He walked, climbed, and waded through snow that was getting deeper by the minute. The animals followed obediently. When his feet regained some feeling, he climbed back into the saddle. "Keep going, fellers."

She'd told John Wesley just what she wanted him to know and nothing else. If she'd told him about the sheriff, he would have had it out with the sheriff, and that would have ruined everything. No, she blamed it all on the Earl of Ravenshire. She had John Wesley believing that some English earl was behind Josh's murder and everything else that had gone wrong.

He'd swallowed it. He'd swallowed every word of it, and walked into a sorry mess he wished to God he'd stayed out of.

Riding in the dark, snow blowing behind him, cold numbing his feet, hands and face, he cursed himself. At first silently, then out loud. Then louder until he was yelling at the top of his voice:

"JOHN WESLEY BUDEEN, YOU AIN'T GOT THE BRAINS GOD GAVE A CHICKEN. IF THERE'S ANY JUSTICE IN THIS WORLD YOU'LL DIE RIGHT HERE. THAT'S WHY IT'S SNOWING, YOU'RE TOO DAMNED DUMB TO LIVE, THAT'S WHY."

Somehow it made him feel better. Yelling made his heart beat faster, his pulse quicken, his blood circulate better. He yelled until he was hoarse. Then he tried to make excuses for himself. If he hadn't been so desperate, if he'd had any choice, a fighting chance, anything, he wouldn't have come on this trip. Aw hell, there's no excuse for being so dumb.

"JOHN WESLEY, YOU'RE A DUMB SHIT. THAT'S ALL THERE IS TO IT. YOU'RE JUST A STUPID, EMPTY-HEADED, BRAINLESS WONDER. THE GODDAM CHICKENS AND SHEEP ARE GENIUSES COMPARED TO YOU."

His voice bounced back to him. The echo came from the west. That's where all those castle-sized boulders were, those boulders that were above timberline. Maybe, just maybe he was at the top of the pass.

CHAPTER 25

It was downhill from here. But it wasn't going to be easy. Snow was a good six inches deep now and getting deeper. The wind was blowing snow, and it was hitting him in the face, blinding him. Not that it mattered. He couldn't see anything anyway. "Hell," he muttered, "I couldn't find my ass with both hands." He urged his animals on. They were glad to be doing downhill.

Remembering that he had to turn west a mile or so and then switch back to the east to get on the trail, he reined his horse to the right. All he could do was hope. Then another problem came up.

Cursing himself again, he knew he should have pulled the iron shoes off his horses' hooves before he'd started this trip. The bottom of horses' hooves were concave and the shoes created more concavity. Snow balled up in them. His horses were walking on four snowballs. Footing in the mountains was treacherous enough in dry weather, and now he was in danger of ending up at the bottom of a hill with horses on top of him. No animal could keep its footing walking on snowballs.

Sure enough, his horse slipped and fell on its side. John Wesley's right leg was trapped under it. "Get up," he yelled, "Get off of me." The horse scrambled up. John Wesley discovered the snow had padded his fall and he wasn't hurt. He groped his way back into the saddle. He kept his feet out of the stirrups and hung onto the saddle horn.

"Keep going, feller," he said. "Do the best you can."

Now he was riding with his heart in his throat. Every time the horse slipped, he was ready to throw himself off. Only, he didn't know which way to fall. Were they on the side of a hill? Under a hill? On top of a ridge? It was so dark he couldn't even see his horse's ears. The wind was howling off a ridge somewhere behind him and snow was sticking to his hat and mackinaw. His feet and hands were freezing. His face was numb.

Men die in these hills. That was the thought going through his mind. It's a long way down. The snow is getting deeper. It will get so deep the horses can't get through it. We'll be snowbound, and if we don't freeze to death we'll starve.

"Keep going, fellers. If we're gonna die let's die trying."

Rich people could afford leather gloves with wool liners. And rubber overboots. They could afford sheepskin coats. The goddam working men who needed those kind of clothes couldn't afford it. Aw hell, John Wesley, you're feeling sorry for yourself. Quit it.

He could wrap the reins around the saddle horn and put his hands in his mackinaw pockets. But then he wouldn't be able to guide the horse. He could get down and walk to keep his feet from freezing. Walk, hell. With his luck he'd fall off a cliff or something. The horses could see in the dark. Even if they didn't know where they were going, they wouldn't fall off the side of a mountain.

The horse slipped again, but stayed right side up. All John Wesley could do was hang on and hope. Slipped again, slid down onto its haunches. This was suicide.

He reined up, got down and working by feel, picked up the horse's left forefoot. Yep, the snow was balled up in there. His fingers were so numb they almost couldn't get his pocket knife open. Finally, he pried open the longest blade and used it to dig the snow out of the bottom of the horse's foot. Then he went to the right side and did the same to the right forefoot. The horse could walk better now, but not for long. The snow would pack in there again. John Wesley waved his arms, stamped his feet and got mounted. They hadn't gone five hundred yards when the horse's forefeet slipped from under it again.

John Wesley was ready this time and he fell clear. He got a face full of snow and lost his hat. Cussing, with the wind blowing through his hair, feeling his body heat going out through the top of his head, he groped in the dark until he found the hat. It was full of snow, and he shook it out and clamped it on tight.

While he was on the ground, he stamped his feet and waved his arms, and got an idea. The mule. Mules have better feet than horses and he'd never had to shoe this one. Not only that, mules had a stronger survival instinct. He'd seen mules so tangled up in harness they couldn't move without tearing hell out of things. Horses would have panicked. The mules just stood there and waited for a human to untangle them. If humans could get fast action out of them, everybody would be riding mules.

"All right, my long-eared friend," he said as he groped his way to the mule. "Let's see if you can do any better." Working by feel again, he got the two horses tied behind the mule and got himself up and into the crossbuck saddle. It was damned uncomfortable, but he could stand it. He had only a halter to guide the mule, but it didn't matter. He didn't know which way to guide it anyhow.

Touching the animal's sides with his spurs, he got it moving. The horses followed. He believed they did. He couldn't see them, but he felt the lead rope tighten.

Snow was up to the animals' knees now, and still falling. It was a major storm. A blizzard. Strangely, instead of worrying about survival he thought about his cattle and horses down in the basin. They would drift, and he'd have to do some riding to find them and bring them back to their home country. It gave him something to think about besides the danger he was in. He was tired of puzzling over Valerie Mitchell and her busted scheme.

The mule's back dipped and swayed. He felt it turn left, go a couple hundred yards and turn back right. Reaching down he patted the animal on the neck. "Good boy. Head for home, my ugly long-eared friend." The horse behind him slipped down and jerked the lead rope. The mule pulled it to its feet and kept going. John Wesley shifted his weight from one hind cheek to the other in the uncomfortable crossbuck saddle. He'd be better off walking, but he didn't know which way to go. The mule seemed to know. It was going home.

It stopped.

"Come on, feller," John Wesley pleaded. "Go on." He touched

its sides with his spurs. It backed up a step. "What the hell's the matter? Go on." He touched it with the spurs again. The mule turned hard left and slid downhill, all four feet braced. The horses behind balked, and the lead rope tied to the pack saddle pulled the mule off its feet and onto its side. John Wesley rolled clear and lost his hold on the halter rope. He stood, but couldn't see a thing. Horses grunted, and he guessed that all three animals were sliding downhill. He took a step and his feet went out from under him and he slid himself. Slid on the seat of his pants. Came to a stop against an animal. The animal was down and struggling to get to its feet. John Wesley was almost under its feet. He crawled on his hands and knees as fast as he could crawl to get out of the way of hard hooves.

He could hear the animals grunt and scramble and he could hear saddle leather creak. Then the only thing he heard was the animals breathing hard from exertion. And the wind. The wind was blowing snow and screaming like a drunk Indian among the trees and boulders.

Fearful of falling off a steep hill, he groped carefully and found a horse. It was standing. Moving slowly, testing the ground before he put each foot down, he found a saddle on its back. The lead rope was tight, which meant it was tied to another animal. It too was standing, sides heaving, carrying a saddle. Stumbling in the dark, he found the mule.

"Are you hurt, feller?" He got ahead of it, feeling his way with his feet, and pulled on the halter. It stepped forward. "Thank the Lord." John Wesley got back in the saddle. It occurred to him he could take the crossbuck saddle off the mule and put a riding saddle in its place. No, on second thought, a riding saddle without a breaching would crawl up onto the mule's neck going downhill. Mules had narrower withers. And he didn't want to try to take the breeching off the pack saddle and put it on a riding saddle in the dark.

To hell with it. A sore ass was the least of his worries.

"What happened, feller? What did we slide off of? Well, let's see if we can go any farther." The mule moved on and the horses followed.

How much longer until daylight? he wondered. Couldn't be much longer. The way the snow was blowing he wouldn't be able to see much in the daylight either. Well, he could at least see something.

Come on daylight.

The mule's back dipped and swayed. The horses slipped and slid behind them.

He was first aware that daylight was coming when he realized he could see the mule's ears. Barely. Its ears were flopping lifelessly. It was walking with slow short steps. Slow and careful. The snow was falling so hard the country ahead of him looked like a solid white sheet. The whole world was white. Looking back, he saw the two horses, dumbly, blindly coming along behind. Being pulled along. Their backs, the saddles, were covered with snow. Where in this cold white range of mountains were they? He had no idea. Everything looked the same. Nothing but snow.

He could cut the two horses loose, pull the saddles off and just turn them loose. Maybe they would find their way down. Maybe not. Maybe the mule could travel better without having to pull the horses along.

No, he'd keep trying and maybe they would all get down.

The mule plodded along. John Wesley didn't try to hurry it. He knew the animal was bone weary because he was having to hang onto the saddle himself. How good it would be just to fall off and lie in the soft snow and sleep. Sleep would come quickly and it would be sweet. Lordy, how he'd like to sleep. Yeah, sleep would be so nice...so soft...so...

With a snort, he came awake just as he felt himself slipping down. He grabbed hold of the saddle and pulled himself erect. Mumbling through stiff lips, he said, "Damn. Can't have that. That would be fatal." He realized that something had awakened him, and he wondered what. And then he knew. It was the mule's ears.

The long ears that had been flopping lifelessly, were now straight up. The mule was walking faster. It had seen something. Seen or heard or smelled something.

John Wesley's face was so cold he could only mumble, "Wha' issit, fell'? We close to home?"

Squinting through the blowing and falling snow, he tried to find a landmark, something recognizable, and he suddenly realized they were on the trail above his homestead. They were close to the spot where he'd first seen Valerie Mitchell.

He raised his face to the sky and licked the snow off his lips. He yelled, first in a strangled voice, then louder, "PRAISE THE LORD, WE'RE GONNA LIVE, FELLERS! WE'RE GONNA MAKE IT. PRAISE THE LORD!" In a quieter tone, he added, "And God bless this jackass."

CHAPTER 26

In two more hours, they were at the bottom of the mountains, down in the basin. The snow wasn't so deep here, but it was still coming down. John Wesley guessed the storm had started on the north slope and had worked its way south. He got off the mule and walked, feeling as if he had lead weights on his feet. It wasn't much farther. But, boy, walking was hard work. In places, where the wind had piled it up, the snow was a good four feet deep, and in other places the wind had cleared most of the snow off the ground. Moving painfully, he made his way around the deep drifts. The ground was frozen hard.

It seemed he was never going to get there. He forced himself to keep walking, stumbling, hoping to get some feeling back in his feet. Windblown snow shortened visibility to only a few yards, and once he veered off in the wrong direction. The mule balked. It made him stop and think, try to see ahead. Changing directions, he stumbled on. And finally they were there.

A force was lifted from John Wesley when he got inside the stock shelter where the wind couldn't pound him. He almost collapsed there and had to order himself to stay right side up. The mule and the horses crowded in beside him. Icicles were hanging from the long hair on their bellies. The wind howled around the corners. He leaned against a corner post and tried to figure out what to do next.

Here, the animals were safe. They had shelter and he could throw some hay to them. As for himself, he had no cabin to get into, but he could wrap up in his blankets, get warm and wait out the storm.

Then what?

He had nothing to eat. The storm could go on for days. He couldn't just lie here in his blankets that long. He wanted to sit down, lie down, but he had to go on.

"Sorry, fellers," he said as he led the three animals out of the corral, back into the battering wind. "Only about five more miles. There's feed and a windbreak there."

Walking, stumbling, he wasn't sure he was doing the smart thing. His animals had traveled about as far as they could travel in the snow. He had traveled as far as he could travel. He walked until he felt a tingling in his toes, figured the blood was circulating now, and got back on the mule. The mule plodded along, long ears flopping. The wind was relentless. Snow flew horizontally. John Wesley pulled the collar of his mackinaw as high as it would go, and his hat as low as it would go and ducked his head to keep the snow from pelting him in the face. When his feet went numb again, he got down and walked.

At mid-afternoon he saw a dim outline of something ahead. Snowfall all but obliterated it. He wiped his eyes with the back of his hand and squinted, trying to see through the blowing snow. It was something big. It was Josh Bennett's house. Back on the mule now, he rode up to the corrals and the three-sided shed. Getting off was easy. He fell off.

His mind barely registered the fact that a horse was in the corral, eating hay out of a manger. And when he stumbled his way out of the corral to the house, he was only barely aware that a one-horse buggy was parked near the door.

The door was latched from the inside. John Wesley tried to yell, but could only croak. He kicked at the door. When it opened, he fell through.

It took a while for his mind to clear, and he found himself on his knees on a wooden floor. There were feet near him. Small feet in high buttoned shoes. Slowly, he stood, blinked, and stared. It was a woman. A young woman.

She spoke, a little fearfully, "Who...who are you?"

His face was so stiff he could barely get the words out. "John...Wesley...Budeen."

"Oh." She seemed relieved. "You're Mr. Budeen. Mr. Weston at the bank told me you were taking care of the ranch."

Swaying, he feared he was going to collapse. "Yeah."

"Well, Mr. Budeen, come over by the stove and sit where you can get warm. There's a terrible storm out there. What were you doing out there?"

He didn't try to answer, but went to the kitchen stove and held his hands over it. A fire was popping in the stove. Warmth crept into his hands, and soon his face was no longer numb.

"Someone was thoughtful enough to store a good supply of firewood in here. Was that you, Mr. Budeen?"

"Yeah, uh..." he took a longer look at her. She was in her mid-twenties, dark hair, in a long wool dress. A heavy wool shawl was draped over her shoulders and held together in front with a big safety pin. Something about her face was familiar. She was pretty.

"Mr. Weston told me you worked at times for my father. He said I owe you some money. I'll certainly pay you, Mr. Budeen, as soon as I can get back to town and to the bank."

"You're...?" He couldn't believe it.

"Yes. Josh Bennett was my father. I've been told that the two of you were the best of friends."

The family portrait on the dresser in the bedroom, the little girl. He frowned at her, and stuttered again, "You're...the one in the picture?"

"In that picture in there? Yes, I am. That picture was taken a long time ago."

"Oh." He didn't know what else to say, but he couldn't take his eyes off her. She couldn't be. She could be. Yeah, the more he looked at her the more resemblance he saw. The wide eyes and the firm round chin.

"Mr. Budeen, I'll put the coffeepot on. I'll bet you're hungry. What were you doing out there? Why don't you take your coat off and your boots, too. You must be frozen."

"Well, I, uh, I've got some horses outside and I've got to take care of them."

"Get warm first."

"I'm all right. I'll be right back." He couldn't rest until the animals were off-saddled and fed, and he went to the door, opened it, and went out into the cold wind and snow.

The wind pushed and pounded on him, but his feet and fingers worked better now as he pulled the saddles off that horses and the mule, and carried hay from the stack behind the stock shelter. "It's gonna be a long winter, fellers. Stuff yourselves while you can." He patted the mule on the shoulder. "Boy, do I owe you."

Back in house, she had the coffeepot on the stove and it was percolating. "Take off your coat, Mr. Budeen, and your boots. I'll fry some bacon and see what else I can find to eat. There isn't much, but surely we can find something."

He didn't want to take his boots off in front of a lady, but he had to get his feet warm. He wished his socks were clean. She didn't seem to notice. They didn't talk again until he had a cup of steaming coffee in his hands, and could smell the bacon frying in an iron skillet. Nothing in the world could have tasted or smelled better.

She sat in a chair at the table. "Mr. Budeen, I've been told that you have a ranch east of here somewhere."

"Yeah, uh, I've got some cattle and horses, but no place to live. My cabin burned down a few days ago."

"Oh, my. And you were staying here until you can build another one?"

"Yeah, that's it, but now that you're here, I'll find someplace else." He had no idea where he would stay.

"Oh, that won't be necessary. I'll stay in town. I don't think I want to make the trip today, however, unless the storm blows over."

"Are you gonna sell this plaice, Miss Bennett?" He wondered if she had a married name.

"No. Not yet, anyhow. I've always wanted to live on a ranch. My father didn't want me here, but now..." Her voice trailed off.

He understood. Josh Bennett wouldn't want a young woman here. Not even his daughter. He couldn't swear, take a bath, or anything with his daughter around. He wanted to ask how she happened to be here during a storm, but he didn't know how to do it. He didn't have to.

"I came out this morning in a rented buggy. It was foolish of me. Mr. Howser at the livery said a storm was coming from the north, over the mountains, but I thought I could get back ahead of it. It came on very suddenly. I managed to get the harness off the horse and feed it some hay. Thank heavens you'd chopped some firewood." She stood and turned the bacon over in the skillet. When she sat down again, she said, "By the way, my name is Charlene. Charlene Bennett. When I was growing up in Amarillo my friends called me Charlie."

Then she wasn't married.

"Obviously, I don't know how to work a ranch, Mr. Budeen, and I'm hoping you..." He interrupted.

"John Wesley. That's what my friends call me."

She smiled. A pretty smile. "Fine. John Wesley it is. As I was saying, I'm hoping you will continue looking after the ranch. I'll pay you, of course. And you can stay here until you get another cabin built. Stay all winter if you want."

The bacon was ready, and she served it in a tin plate with thick slices of bread and apple butter. The bread was stale, but hadn't started molding yet, and he ate his fill. He felt good now, better than he'd felt in a long time. She watched him eat, went to the window and looked out.

"It's still snowing. How long do you think it will last?"

"You never know. It could go on for a couple of days."

"Oh my. That means I'll have to spend the night here."

"More than likely."

"Mr. Budeen, John Wesley, do you mind sleeping on the floor in the kitchen?"

"No. I've got a bedroll outside. I'll bring it in when I go out to see to the horses again. Don't worry, I've slept on the floor a lot of nights."

"My father trusted you, John Wesley, and I'll trust you, too."

She'd called him John Wesley. Not John or Johnnie. He liked that. He took another sip of coffee, leaned back in his chair, and straightened his knees. A contented sigh came out of him.

Maybe it wouldn't be such a long winter after all.

THE END

Be sure to check out the next novel in
Doyle Trent's Tales of the Old Wild West series:

DODGE CITY TRAIL

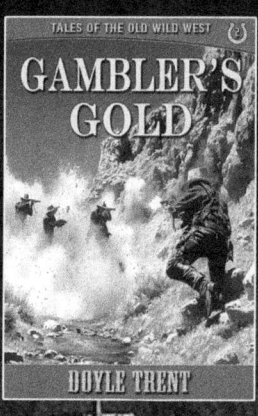

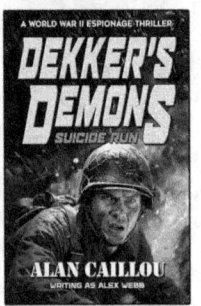

ADDITIONAL ACTION & ADVENTURE
FROM ALAN CAILLOU

FROM FANTASY AND SCIENCE FICTION
AUTHOR ROLAND J. GREEN
THREE EPIC SERIES

FROM CALIBER BOOKS IN PAPERBACK AND EBOOK

CALIBER COMICS GOES TO WAR!
HISTORICAL AND MILITARY THEMED GRAPHIC NOVELS

**WORLD WAR ONE:
MO MAN'S LAND**

ISBN: 9781635298123

*A look at World War 1 from
the French trenches as they
faced the Imperial German
Army.*

**CORTEZ AND THE FALL
OF THE AZTECS**

ISBN: 9781635299779

*Cortez battles the Aztecs
while in search of Inca
gold.*

**TROY:
AN EMPIRE UNDER SIEGE**

ISBN: 9781635298635

*Homer's famous The Iliad and
the Trojan War is given a
unique human perspective
rather than from the God's.*

WITNESS TO WAR

ISBN: 9781635299700

*WW2's Battle of the Bulge
is seen up close by an
embedded female war
reporter.*

THE LINCOLN BRIGADE

ISBN: 9781635298222

*American volunteers head
to Spain in the 1930s to
fight in their civil war
against the fascist regime.*

**EL CID:
THE CONQUEROR**

ISBN: 9780982654996

*Europe's greatest warrior
attempts to unify Spain
against invading foreign
and domestic armies.*

WINTER WAR

ISBN: 9780985749392

*At the outbreak of WW2
Finland fights against an
invading Soviet army.*

**ZULUNATION:
END OF EMPIRE**

ISBN: 9780941613415

*The global British Empire
and far-reaching influence
is threatened by a Zulu
uprising in southern Africa.*

AIR WARRIORS: WORLD WAR ONE #V1 - V4   *Take to the skys of WW1 as various fighter aces tell their harrowing stories.*
ISBN: 9781635297973 (V1), 9781635297980 (V2), 9781635297997 (V3), 9781635298000 (V4)

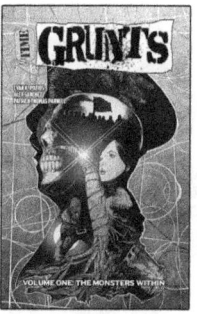